MUMFIE'S MAGIC BOX

One friend of Mumfie's wrote in *The Listener* 'I predict for Mumfie a small niche among the immortals.'

This might have turned his head had he not been uncertain what exactly a 'niche' was. In any case, since then he scarcely had a moment to spare; adventures fell thick and fast.

Other MUMFIE books

HERE COMES MUMFIE
MUMFIE'S UNCLE SAMUEL
THE WANDERINGS OF MUMFIE

and published by CAROUSEL BOOKS

Katharine Tozer

MUMFIE'S MAGIC BOX

With illustrations by the Author

CAROUSEL BOOKS
A DIVISION OF TRANSWORLD PUBLISHERS LTD

MUMFIE'S MAGIC BOX

A CAROUSEL BOOK 0 552 52068 3

Originally published in Great Britain by
John Murray Ltd.

PRINTING HISTORY
John Murray edition published 1938
Carousel edition published 1977

This book is set in 12pt. Monotype Baskerville

Carousel Books are published by
Transworld Publishers Ltd.,
Century House, 61–63 Uxbridge Road,
Ealing, London W5 5SA
Made and printed in Great Britain by
Cox & Wyman Ltd., London, Reading and Fakenham

For Margaret

not of course forgetting Piglet

CHAPTER ONE

THE lane wound white and dusty between high hedges bright with spring flowers. It was deserted save for two figures who walked along side by side; one lean and rakish, the other small and stumpy.

'Let's go in this field,' said Scarecrow, stopping to lean over a gate. He flapped his hat idly at a blue butterfly.

'No. There's a bull in that one – a very fierce snorting sort of bull. Let's go on round the bend, Scarecrow, there's a lovely field farther on – it's got some pigs in it – they was ever so little the other day – in fact, their mama was only just putting the curls into their tails.'

Mumfie looked up hopefully.

'Well, I think this field will do.' Scarecrow looked

down at his boots. 'I think I've got a corn.' He rubbed his left foot against the leg of his blue trousers. Mumfie tugged at his arm.

'Do come, Scarecrow. It's not much farther on, and besides I *believe* one of those pigs was rather peculiar.'

'There's nothing peculiar about pigs except bacon,' said Scarecrow rather severely because his foot was hurting, but he turned round and began walking down the lane. Mumfie trotted happily beside him.

'This is the field,' he said presently. He scrambled over the gate and made his way towards a sty, where a large pig was lying surrounded by her family.

'Well, I don't see anything peculiar about any of those,' said Scarecrow. 'They just look like ordinary pigs to me.'

But Mumfie was busy counting.

'There's only eight here.' He ticked them off on his fingers. 'I'm sure there was nine the other day, though one of them was so very small that perhaps it's got . . .' He was interrupted by a rather sad sound coming from somewhere behind the sty; a sound between a squeak and a sob. Mumfie trotted round to have a look, and there, sitting by itself in a very woebegone attitude, was an extremely small pink pig. It did not move as Mumfie came up, but looked up at him sadly.

'Oh dear, oh dear!' said Mumfie. 'I've found it, Scarecrow, but I'm afraid it isn't very happy. What's the matter?' he asked kindly, sitting himself down beside it.

'Nuffin,' snuffled the small pig. A large tear splashed off its nose and fell into a pool at its feet.

'But you really does look mis'able.' Mumfie looked concerned. 'Can't we do anything to help?'

'Well, that certainly *is* a peculiar pig,' cried Scare-

6

crow who had just come up. 'Why, bless me if it hasn't got . . .'

'SH . . .' Mumfie made faces at him to be quiet, he was afraid of hurting the little creature's feelings.

'It's all right,' said the pig. 'I know what you were going to say. That's just the trouble. I mean THEY'RE just the trouble. You see, none of my brothers and sisters have got any – any of these.'

It stood up, and rather miserably flapped a little pair of blue wings that were set neatly behind its ears.

Mumfie stared in open-eyed admiration.

'But I think they's lovely!' he cried. 'I had a pair of water wings once, just like that. Do they come off?' he asked hopefully.

'No,' said the pig. 'Not nohow. I sometimes wish they did.'

'Can you fly?' Mumfie jumped up and down. 'Oo, it must be fun. I wish I had a pair.'

'I can a little.' The pig brightened at this admiration. 'I'm not very good at it. You see, my brothers and sisters don't seem to approve of flying. They won't ever let me get far off the ground. They comes up and catches hold of my tail. Which is worrying – when you're learning. Oh dear, oh dear!' It began to look sad again. 'I do wish I was an ordinary pig.'

'Oo, please would you fly just a little way for me to see?' begged Mumfie.

The pig looked nervously towards two of its brothers, who had wuffled round the corner of the sty, and were regarding the proceedings intently.

'I'd rather not if you don't mind,' it said unhappily.

'Cowardy cowardy CUSTARD!' squeaked the two brothers, frisking their hind legs into the air. 'Cowardy cowardy . . .'

'I'm NOT!' stamped the small pig. 'I'm not, and I'll show you!'

It flitted its wings and rose in a rather wobbly manner a little way off the ground.

With a squeal of delight the two brothers rushed forward and caught hold of it by its tail, which came uncurled, and streamed out in a straight line behind it.

'Oh! Oh!' cried the small pig, flapping wildly. Then it overbalanced and fell with a bump to the ground.

'Here, none of that!' Scarecrow seized hold of a pig in each hand by the end of their curly tails. He swung them up into the air.

'Bet YOU can't do it,' he jeered. 'Now go on, and let's see YOU fly down.'

'Oh no! Help, help! We'll tell Mother!' shrieked the brothers, kicking frantically.

8

'Cowardy cowardy CUSTARD!' sang Mumfie, as Scarecrow let them both go. They bounced to the ground and went scuttering off to their mother as fast as their short legs would carry them.

The small pig giggled happily as it watched their flight. 'Oh, that was kind of you,' it said. 'You see, I really do want to fly, and if I don't practise now my wings won't grow properly. But it's really dreadfully difficult with them hanging on to my tail.'

'How did you come by your wings in the first place?' asked Scarecrow. 'Any more like you in the family? Distant relatives, I mean?'

'Well, I don't know,' said the little pig thoughtfully. 'You see, this isn't really my own family. I'm sort of adopted. I can't remember where my proper family is, I was so very small when I left, though I do have funny dreams at times, when I can remember places not a bit like this field. Oh dear,' it sighed, 'I do wish I could find my own family. I don't think I'm going to enjoy being an ordinary pig at all. You see, I don't *feel* ordinary, and I don't *look* it, and if I can't learn to fly I shall just have to stay on the ground – and that will be really very dull.'

It looked as though it would begin crying again at any moment.

Mumfie poked Scarecrow.

'Oh, Scarecrow, don't you think we might be able to find his family for him? After all, it shouldn't be difficult. Pigs with wings do stand out. We might walk round all the fields where there are pigs and see if we could find any.'

'We might,' said Scarecrow. 'But I don't believe there ARE any more. Besides, there's the small matter of my bad toe.'

'Yes, but, Scarecrow, we can't just leave him here in the field for his brothers to bully. If he was adopted, then his foster mother probably knows where he came from. I shall go and ask her.'

He stumped off to where the old pig was lying lazily with her nose buried in a nice piece of wet mud.

'Excuse me, madam,' began Mumfie very politely, 'but could you tell me . . .'

'Squaumph!' said the pig.

'I beg your pardon?'

'Squaumph!' said the pig again. It closed its eyes and appeared to be going to sleep.

'It's no good talking,' said the little pig shyly, coming up. 'She doesn't approve of it – says pigs should be seen but not heard.'

'Well, that settles it,' said Mumfie decidedly.

'You can't go on living here without any conversation. If you go on like this much longer all you will be able to say is SQUAUMPH! – and that wouldn't do at all.

You'd better come along with us and we'll see what we can do about finding your family. Won't we, Scarecrow? By the way,' he said with a rather worried expression, 'what sort of things do you eat?'

'Those sort of things.' It pointed to some rather muddy-looking turnips. 'But they don't agree with me. That's probably why I'm so small.'

'Well,' said Mumfie hopefully, 'p'r'aps Mumfie Mashes would agree with you. Mumfie Mash with Scarecrow Stuffing. Anyway, we can try. Come along while she's still asleep.'

'Perhaps,' said Scarecrow, as they walked quietly across the field, 'if you were to tell us something about those dreams of yours, it might help.'

'Well, let me see,' began the little pig, who in its excitement was taking short flights into the air. 'Let me see if I can remember.'

CHAPTER TWO

'HE distinctly remembers an island,' said Mumfie, as he and Scarecrow sat in Selina's room waiting for her to come in and put them to bed.

'I can't see how he can have just dreamt it all. I mean about that nice old gentleman – and the house at the bottom of the orchard.'

'Yes, I know,' frowned Scarecrow. 'But he doesn't seem to have any idea as to whereabouts the island is.'

'Well, perhaps if we went down to the beach we might find someone who knows of an island where there are flying pigs. Should we go now, Scarecrow? We could be back again before Selina comes in.'

'We might,' said Scarecrow, who was trying to mend a hole in his sock by tying a piece of string round it. 'What shall we do about him. Shall we wake him?'

He pointed to where the small pig was lying curled up and fast asleep in the middle of Selina's nightdress-case.

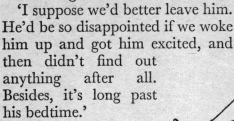

'I suppose we'd better leave him. He'd be so disappointed if we woke him up and got him excited, and then didn't find out anything after all. Besides, it's long past his bedtime.'

'Yes, I know. But just supposing . . .' Mumfie looked inquiringly at Scarecrow.

'Oh, I see what you mean. In that case we'd better take him along.' Scarecrow finished the sock and tried it on.

'Oh dear, that's made it a bit short in the toe. It also makes a nobble in my boot – which is not the best thing to walk on. Still, I've had 'em five years now, so I suppose I can't complain.'

He got up and went over to the mantelpiece where he started to open his money-box.

'You never know,' he said, shaking out a sixpence. 'Always as well to have something in your pocket.' He rattled out a penny and three of Mumfie's farthings. 'That ought to be enough. Oh, and I think I'll take a box of matches – and, Mumfie, you'd better see you've got a pencil and paper because you nearly always need to write a note. It does seem a pity to wake Pinkey, though.'

He looked at the little pig, who was snoring happily. They had christened him Pinkey because he was so very pink that it really suited him.

'I'll wrap him up in one end of my muffler then p'r'aps he won't wake.'

Mumfie picked up the small pig, who stirred and grunted, but did not properly wake up. He fetched himself a piece of letter-paper and a stub of pencil and then they crept out down the passage and out of the back door.

The trees stood dark against a pale green evening sky. Mumfie picked some night scented stock and put it in his buttonhole. 'It smells lovely,' he whispered. They crept out of the garden and down the lane towards the sea-shore.

Mumfie felt happy and bouncy inside. He sang a little song to himself and snuffed at his flower. The lane began to get sandy under their feet; before them rose the dunes, a fresh evening breeze from the sea rustling amongst their stiff grasses. The little pig stirred and began talking to itself in its sleep.

'What is it saying?' asked Scarecrow, stopping to listen. 'It sounded like geography to me.'

'I don't know,' said Mumfie. 'But it can't be that 'cos he's too young to have learnt any – why, I've only just begun it myself.'

Pinkey moved again.

'Latitudesoansolongitudesoanso,' he said quite clearly, then grunted and went soundly to sleep again.

'Well, I'll be blowed!' Scarecrow looked surprised. 'Rather intelligent for his age. Mumfie, you don't suppose that could be something to do with his island? He might have heard somebody say it. I didn't, and you didn't. And I'm sure the pigs in his field know nothing about it. Anyhow, it's worth trying; the best thing we can do is to go along the beach and see if there's anyone about who can tell us where Latitude So-and-so, Longitude So-and-so is.'

They walked along the smooth wet sand for some way, whilst dusk came down around them.

'Let's make towards the wreck,' suggested Mumfie. 'There's generally a few fishermen around there digging up worms for bait. This part of the shore seems quite deserted.'

It was by now getting quite dark; Mumfie, who was not looking where he was going, stumbled into some driftweed and fell on his nose. Pinkey tumbled out of the muffler, but it was so long after his bedtime that he did not wake up.

'Here, let me have him for a bit,' said Scarecrow. 'You want to watch where you're going, Mumfie.' He put Pinkey carefully into his pocket.

'Is that the wreck?' asked Mumfie, pointing to a dark mass that loomed ahead of them.

Scarecrow peered through the darkness.

'No, I don't think so. I don't know what it is – it doesn't look like a wreck to me, but there was nothing else of that size here this morning.'

'I think we'd better go and look.' Mumfie made his way towards it.

'Oo, Scarecrow, it looks like a mountain. I don't think I likes the look of it.'

'It can't be a mountain right in the middle of the beach, besides mountains don't grow up overnight. My goodness, but I believe it is, though. Oh, and it's all slippery!' He poked the mountain cautiously with his finger.

'And it's alive!' said Mumfie, touching it.

'Oh, and my goodness me.' He walked round it. 'I

believe it's got an eye. Is that an eye up there, Scare-crow?'

'Certainly it's an eye,' said the mountain. 'And what's more, it's MY eye.'

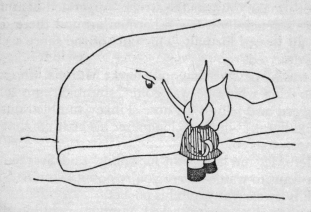

'Oh mercy!' cried Mumfie, running back a few yards. 'Did YOU say that, Scarecrow?'

'No, IT did. I think we'd better go and find that wreck, Mumfie.' He began to beat a hasty retreat.

'Oh, don't go away,' said the mountain. 'For good-ness' sake don't go off and leave me now – just when I thought assistance was on the way.'

Mumfie and Scarecrow came back.

'Are you in trouble?' asked Mumfie. He did not quite know which part of the mountain to address, so walked round until he found the eye again.

'Yes I am. In terrible trouble. I've got washed up owing to a slight oversight on my part, and if the tide doesn't soon come up and wash me down again it will be all up with me.'

'He doesn't seem to know whether he wants to be up or down,' muttered Scarecrow.

'What are you, anyway? I don't think I've seen anything like you before.'

'I am a Whale, of course,' said the monster rather feebly. 'And I can't recollect ever having seen anything like you before. Oh dear, oh dear, I don't feel well.'

'Poor thing.' Mumfie looked puzzled.

'I don't know how we're going to get him into the sea again without help. He looks far too heavy to push.'

'Well, there's no harm in trying. The beach looks pretty sloping there, and he's so slippery that if we once got him started he might slide. Look out,' he said to the whale. 'We're going to push you.'

They began to push, but it was just like trying to move a mountain. Mumfie was becoming quite purple in the face when he noticed something projecting at one side of the whale.

'Look,' he said, 'there's a boulder or something in front of him – if we could pull that away he might slide down.'

The object proved to be one of the fishermen's dinghies, which was firmly wedged under the whale's snout. The next ten minutes they spent in frantically digging the sand away from under the boat so that presently there was a sucking noise and they were able to drag it away from the whale.

'Look out!' shrieked Scarecrow, dragging Mumfie to one side. 'He's moving.'

The whale had begun slowly to slip forward. They rushed behind it pushing with all their might, until they felt the water lapping round their ankles. Mumfie stopped pushing, and darted back in time to avoid a large wave that came tumbling in.

17

'That's all right,' said the whale, swinging broadside on. 'I can manage now. I really am most awfully obliged to you. I wish I could do something for you by way of return.'

'Oh but you could,' said Scarecrow. 'Hang on a minute. I suppose you don't know where Latitude So-and-so, Longitude So-and-so is?'

'I ought to,' replied the whale, 'seeing that it's quite close to where I live.'

'When will you be going home again?' asked Scarecrow eagerly. This seemed almost too good to be true.

'I ought to be getting back now. My mother will be wondering what's happened to me. Well, I can't keep afloat in this shallow water much longer. Sure there's nothing I can do for you?'

'Oh yes!' sang Mumfie and Scarecrow together, 'I suppose you couldn't give us a lift?'

'Lift! Why of course I could. I'd be delighted. As a matter of fact I'm all fitted up as a passenger liner inside – but trade's bad – you wouldn't believe how bad trade is, though no one could complain that I am shaky, AND I've won the blue riband in my time. Just wait 'til I turn the lights on. You'd better fetch the dinghy to bring yourselves aboard.'

Mumfie squealed with excitement as he and Scarecrow raced back to fetch the dinghy. Along the whale's side had appeared a long row of round winking lights.

'Hurry up,' boomed the monster as they brought the boat alongside. 'Catch hold of the ladder and whatever you do don't fall into the sea.'

'What about the dinghy?' bellowed Scarecrow when he had seen Mumfie safely on to the ladder.

'Oh, that's all right. I'll take care of that. I'll make a wave with my tail that will beach her again.'

Scarecrow scrambled up the rope ladder and followed Mumfie through a small doorway. They were no sooner safely inside than they felt the whale shoot forward, and they were cutting through the water at a tremendous speed. Mumfie peeped through a porthole to see pale white breakers at the water's edge disappear behind them in the darkness.

CHAPTER THREE

'OO, look at this lovely little cabin,' said Mumfie happily. He went inside and bounced upon the bunk. 'Have you got Pinkey safe? We'd better put him to bed in that bunk, then we can have this one.'

He scrambled up and made room for Scarecrow, who was busy settling the still sleeping Pinkey. From where they lay they could see through the porthole the dark bowl of the sky, carpeted with a million stars.

'This is lovely,' Mumfie whispered. 'I wonder where we shall be by tomorrow morning.'

'I dunno,' Scarecrow muttered. 'Somewhere where I can dry off, I hope. I got a bit wet getting out of the dinghy.'

'Well, you're not as wet as you got last time,' giggled Mumfie happily. 'Oo, look over there. There's a long line of stars fallen into the sea. They're travelling along on the water the same way as us.'

'Those are not stars, that's another liner like us. I expect they are looking at us through their portholes.' He looked down at Mumfie, who had quite suddenly fallen asleep.

'Well, I might as well take a nap myself,' he muttered. 'We're not likely to be there yet. Wherever that may be.' He curled himself round Mumfie to keep him from slipping about, and was soon fast asleep.

They were wakened by a rumbling sound underneath them, ending in a loud bellow.

' 'Elp!' said Mumfie, springing up in such a fright that he nearly tumbled out of the bunk. ' 'Elp, where am I?' He ran to the porthole and stuck his head out.

'Thought I'd never wake you up,' roared the whale. 'I was almost beginning to think that you'd both fallen overboard in the night.'

'My word, you're in good voice this morning,' grumbled Scarecrow, who had been in the middle of a very pleasant dream.

'Yes, am I not? I feel in very good form this morning. Wonderful what a good swim can do for the constitution. Well, this must be round about where you want to get off; though how I can leave you in mid-ocean I don't know.'

But Mumfie and Scarecrow had run up upon the deck and were looking around them in amazement. The air was hot and hazy under a brilliant sun, the sea lay calm around them rising in a gentle lazy swell, the water looked warm and inviting.

'Wish I'd brought my bathing suit,' said Scarecrow. 'I could almost be persuaded to go in swimming. I say!' he yelled towards the whale's head. 'Are you sure this is the place we're looking for?'

'This is it,' said the whale. 'Near enough. I shall really have to park you soon, you know. It's a long time since supper, and I shall have to see about a little breakfast.'

' 'Hem, breakfast.' Scarecrow licked his lips with his pink tongue. 'That reminds me, it's about time we did a little thinking on the same subject. But what bothers me is that I don't see the sign of any island.' He looked round rather anxiously. 'P'r'aps we haven't gone quite far enough.'

Mumfie shaded his eyes with his hand. 'There's rather a funny patch of mist over there,' he said. 'Maybe that's land getting misty in the morning heat.'

But the whale, who had been lying very still in the water listening to the conversation, suddenly moved so quickly that Scarecrow slithered down into the scuppers and very nearly fell overboard.

'Here, look out!' he was beginning, when the whale interrupted him with something between a snort and a gasp.

'Did I hear you say anything about an *island*?' it asked in a doubtful voice.

'Yes,' answered Scarecrow. 'There should be an island round about here, and that is where we want to land, if you would be so good as to take us inshore.'

'Oh, my goodness. I couldn't do that.' The monster sounded distressed. 'You didn't say anything about the island last night, or I would have told you that right away. I don't know what your business there is, but you'd better give up all idea of landing on that island at once, and let me take you straight home again.'

'Oh, but we MUST get on it. We've a very special

reason. Is there any particular reason why we shouldn't?'

'Yes, indeed there is. I should say so. You must be mad even to think of it.' It rolled about nervously in the water.

Mumfie looked at Scarecrow. 'Ask him what's the matter. I can't think what he's getting so nervous about.'

But the whale when questioned refused to say anything further than that it would on no account land them on the island. What was more, it advised them that if they valued their lives they would not attempt to go anywhere near it.

'*I* wouldn't,' it said. 'And goodness knows I'm big enough to look after myself in most situations.'

Scarecrow looked towards the mist-covered water with apprehension. 'I suppose he knows what he's talking about,' he said doubtfully. 'What do you think, Mumfie?'

'I don't know what to think as he won't say exactly what is the matter. I think we'd better go and see for ourselves,' he said stoutly. 'After all, we can hardly take Pinkey back when we've brought him all this way. How is he, by the way?'

'Splendiferous, thank you,' said Pinkey, who had come up from the cabin unheard by them, and was sniffing around. He began to bounce about on the whale's back, taking short flights into the air. They had never seen him looking so happy. He snuffled his snout into the air, flapped his wings, and pirouetted in a little dance all the way up to the whale's head. Then he fluttered into the air and flew out a little way over the sea. 'Oh, do be careful!' called Mumfie. 'Take care you don't get wobbly and flop in.'

'He's all right.' Scarecrow watched under the shade of his hand. 'He's doing it much better than he ever did before; which all goes to prove that he must be in his native element. Come on, Mumfie, if we can't persuade the whale to take us I think we'd better swim for it. We'll get pretty wet, but it won't take us much time to dry off in this heat. Pinkey, how far do you think you could fly this morning?'

'Oh, miles and miles and miles,' said Pinkey, flying about. 'You watch me.'

'Well, come down, and don't use up all your strength before you need it – water's deceptive and it may be farther off than it looks. Are you ready, Mumfie? Better take your shoes off and put them in my pocket, it will be easier swimming without them – good thing we had so much practice last year.'

Mumfie sat down and took off his shoes. He was looking forward to the swim, the water looked so green and inviting.

'I shall dive in,' he announced. 'Watch me diving, Scarecrow.'

He put his hands before him in a swimming position and dived off into the water, only something happened to the dive in mid-air and he landed very flat on the water with a good deal of splash. Scarecrow dived in after him, and Pinkey flew over their heads.

Gradually the whale became small in the distance. It seemed a shame to leave it in such a sudden manner without even saying good-bye, but there was nothing else to be done. They swam on towards the mist until soon it became wreathed around them and it was hard to see each other in the water.

'How are you getting along, Mumfie?' called Scarecrow anxiously. They seemed to have been swimming

24

for a long time without getting any farther and there was no sign of any land.

'I'm all right,' said Mumfie. 'My arms are a little stiff, and one of my toes feels funny, but I can go on for quite a bit. Where's Pinkey?' he asked, looking up. 'Oh, Scarecrow, I can't see him. PINKEY!' he called out.

A rather breathless squeak came up to them through the mist; they paddled about, treading water until Pinkey came in sight, fluttering rather feebly, and at times almost sinking into the water.

'Oh dear, oh dear,' said Pinkey sadly, 'I'm not so good as I thought I was. It's this fog, it makes my wings so wet they feel just like plum puddings.'

'Never mind,' said Scarecrow cheerfully. 'It can't be far now. You sit on top of my head. You aren't a bit heavy, and it will give you a rest.'

'Thank you, Scarecrow, you are very kind.' Pinkey landed on Scarecrow's hat with a little plop. It was not long before he was curled up and fast asleep.

Mumfie and Scarecrow swam on. They were so tired that they hardly looked where they were going, so that they were amazed to see suddenly tall rocks leaping up at them through the mist, which seemed to be thinner. It wreathed itself about in long curling wisps that licked along the shore like smoke from a wood fire.

'I can feel the land under my feet!' said Scarecrow presently. He began to wade out of the water.

Mumfie stumbled up after him. He found that his legs were all wobbly so that he wanted to fall down. He staggered about, and finally sat down with a bump. 'Oo, my, I do feel peculiar. Wouldn't it be a good plan to take Pinkey off your hat?' he suggested. 'You look a little mad with him perched on the top of your head.'

'My goodness, I'd forgotten all about him. What a good thing he's still there.'

Scarecrow sat down beside Mumfie and they looked around them. The rocks rose behind them creeping up to the edge of a dark pine forest. It was strangely quiet. There was no sound but the water lapping against the pebbles, and Mumfie who was still breathing rather heavily through his trunk from his exertions.

'Well, now what?' said Scarecrow. 'We can't just leave him here on the shore. We'd better find out if he really does live here. I haven't seen any flying pigs about myself; though of course they might have been hidden in the fog. Tell you what, Mumfie, that swim made me mighty hungry.'

'That's it,' said Mumfie decidedly. 'That's what is the matter with me. I was just wondering. I felt very peculiar inside. We'd better see if we can find anything to eat before we do anything else.'

He got up and began to climb carefully up the rocks.

'There might be some berries in these woods,' he called over his shoulder. He stopped suddenly. 'My goodness but it's quiet here. They don't seem very friendly sort of woods, Scarecrow. P'r'aps we'd better walk along the shore for a bit and see if we can get inland without going through them.'

He began to remember the things the whale had suggested about the island. It had a rather hostile feeling – almost as if it resented their landing.

They climbed over the boulders which hemmed in the creek where they had landed, but it was evident that there was no way out unless they took to the water again.

'Well,' said Mumfie, hitching up his belt, 'it looks as if we'll have to go this way. P'r'aps we'll be better when we've had a little food, Scarecrow.'

'P'r'aps we shall,' agreed Scarecrow. He picked up the dozing Pinkey and together they scrambled up towards the woods.

CHAPTER FOUR

THE forest was tall, dark, and very quiet, so that the undergrowth crackling beneath their feet seemed almost alarmingly loud. The trees grew thick and tangled, as if few people ever came that way. Scarecrow went ahead trying to find a path.

'There seems to be some sort of path here,' he called out. 'It's very narrow and twisty, but I think we'd better follow it or we'll probably get lost. Oh dear, but I AM hungry.'

28

Mumfie was looking round for berries to eat; there was a tree covered with bright green fruit, but it was too far above their heads to reach. Mumfie gazed at the berries hungrily. 'Let's wake up Pinkey,' he suggested. 'He could fly up and get us some.'

They woke the sleepy Pinkey, who flew up on to the branch and was just going to pick some of the fruit when he began jumping up and down with excitement.

'I can see smoke over there,' he squeaked. 'I'm sure I can. I s'pecs there's someone living in the forest.'

'It's probably only the mist that hangs around the island,' said Scarecrow. 'It looks far too deserted for anyone to live here. Still, there's no harm in looking.'

They were so excited that they forgot all about the berries. Pinkey fluttered amongst the trees trying to keep the smoke in sight, but the branches were so thick that he had soon to come down. The path was, however, becoming more clearly marked. As they went along they could see signs of the bushes having been cut back to make a small clearing.

'Oh, look!' shouted Mumfie, who had run on ahead, 'I do believe it's a little house.'

Sure enough, there in the clearing before them was a strange little twisted cottage. The smoke they had seen was wreathing up from its single chimney.

Mumfie stumped happily along. He hoped there would be somebody at home, and that it would be about their breakfast time. He was so hungry that he felt to himself just like an empty pillow. He was running up to knock on the door when Scarecrow caught hold of him. 'We'd better be careful,' he cautioned. 'We don't know if the person who lives here is likely to be friendly or not. It might even be a witch, though it certainly doesn't look like a witch's cottage. I'll knock and you and Pinkey stand behind me and be ready to beat a hasty retreat.'

There was no knocker or bell on the door, so he reached up and tapped against it gently. They waited rather nervously, but there was no answer. Scarecrow knocked again, louder this time, but it soon became evident that there was no one at home. They went round to the back of the cottage but there was not a soul about.

'Oh bother,' said Mumfie disappointedly. 'And I did hope there would be someone in, and that they were just going to sit down to their breakfast.' He was so very hungry that he found it quite difficult not to start crying. Scarecrow looked at his woebegone little face, and hitched up his belt in a determined manner.

'Well, as there's nobody at home I think I shall take a look inside,' he sniffed. 'It smells very much to me as if there was some-

thing cooking. There wouldn't be any harm in just looking.'

He went over to the window which was covered over with some flowering plant, and looked inside. It was so dark that he could not make anything out very clearly. He looked disappointed.

'I can't *see* any food,' he said. 'All I can make

30

out is lots and lots of books.' He came back to the front
door and very carefully tried the handle. Rather to his
surprise the door opened easily. He peeped round it,
and then went inside.

'Oh, do be careful, Scarecrow,' said Mumfie,
following him, and holding on to the back of his coat.
'The owner can't be very far off, or they wouldn't
have left the door unlocked. They might come back at
any moment.'

But Scarecrow was not to be deterred; he went on
into the tiny hall. A grandfather clock back in the darkness began to strike. Scarecrow leapt back in a fright,
nearly knocking Mumfie over.

'Bother the thing, it gave me a fright.' They waited
while the clock struck nine. Mumfie peeped about him.
'I likes this house,' he announced. 'It feels rather
friendly. I don't think the owner would mind very
much our being here. Oo, Scarecrow, do you think
that door along there could be the kitchen. It *smells*
rather like the kitchen,' he added hopefully.

Scarecrow pushed open the door and went
in.

They found themselves in a tiny low kitchen, with an
oven in one corner on which something was simmering
gently in a big iron pot. Scarecrow went over to it and
lifted the lid.

'Oh dear, oh dear,' he said, 'this is almost too much.
I do wish they'd come back, then they might invite us
to breakfast.'

But the delicious smell had upset Pinkey entirely; he
broke into a loud wail.

'I'm hungry,' he said. 'Pinkey's hungry.'

'You don't suppose it's *over*-cooked?' suggested
Mumfie hopefully. 'Hadn't we better try it just to see.

Look, there's a big ladle over there. P'r'aps we could take out a few spoonfuls.'

He climbed on a chair and reached for the ladle. The stew was delicious. Scarecrow blew on it to cool it off a little, and they gave some to Pinkey, who ate it greedily and called for more. After four full ladles Scarecrow decided that he had had enough. He really had a very big appetite for so small a pig. He filled it again, and handed it to Mumfie, then went over to the window to see if there was anyone coming.

'Oh my goodness!' said Scarecrow in a voice of such alarm that Mumfie upset some stew all down his nice coat. 'Oh my goodness, that's torn it. There's somebody coming. And what's more, they're coming towards this house. Quick, we'd better get out.'

Mumfie dropped the ladle and they made a rush for the door. They tried the handle, but to their dismay it was firmly shut. There was no time to run through to the front again. They crouched by the window, watching as an old man made his appearance in the clearing. He was a very strange old man with a peculiar cap on his head. He walked in a slow and dignified manner, and clasped a large and dusty-looking book under one arm. He assisted his aged steps with a stout nobbly stick which Scarecrow eyed apprehensively.

'I think he's going round to the front,' he whispered. 'Whatever shall we do?'

'Couldn't we climb out of the window?' suggested Mumfie. He tried it, but it was very stiff; creepers grew across the glass outside and it had evidently not been opened for years. He looked thoughtfully towards the front door, which they had forgotten to shut behind them.

'I think we'd better go and meet him,' he said.

'After all, we have eaten some of his breakfast, and p'r'aps when he hears how very hungry we were he won't be cross.'

'How very hungry I AM,' put in Scarecrow, who had been interrupted before it came to his turn. 'Perhaps you're right, Mumfie. You go first. You're a bit more taking than I am at first sight. Sometimes mistaken people take me for a tramp.' He did up the remaining button on his coat in order to make himself a bit more presentable, and followed Mumfie to the door.

The old man was coming up the path as Mumfie reached the front door. He looked so exceedingly surprised at the sight of anyone in his cottage that he was at a loss for words.

'Oh, sir,' began Mumfie in a trembly voice, 'I do hope you don't mind very much. We waited ever such a long time to see if you would come home, and then we felt so dreadfully hungry that we – oh dear—' He broke off, glancing nervously round at Scarecrow. 'We helped ourselves to some of your stew.' He had to fight very hard to prevent himself from making a sudden dash past the old gentleman and rushing off into the forest just as fast as his legs would carry him. He looked up into a face which, far from being angry, was regarding them in a kindly though rather puzzled manner.

'Dear, dear,' the old man was saying. 'Dear, dear, dear. This is indeed very strange. I am quite unused to visitors these days. It is in fact such a long time since anyone came to see me that I find myself quite at a loss. Come inside, come inside. If you are hungry then of course you must have something to eat.'

He shepherded them back into the cottage and into the room at which Scarecrow had first peeped.

'You must forgive me if I seem inquisitive,' he said, 'but you are strangers to these parts, are you not?'

'Yes, we are, sir,' answered Mumfie, gazing round in admiration at the books with which the entire walls of the room were lined.

'What a lot of books you've got, sir. Have any of them got pictures?'

The old professor smiled indulgently.

'Some of them have pictures,' he said. 'Though I fear that you would find them a little dull. Have you come a long distance?'

Mumfie began to explain about Pinkey, ably assisted by Scarecrow, who at the old man's kindness was beginning to feel quite at home. They looked round for Pinkey, but he must have stayed in the kitchen. Mumfie trotted out to find him, so did not notice that the professor's usually mild expression had changed, as they told their story, to one of considerable alarm.

'Did you say a *winged* pig?' he asked anxiously. 'A very young pig with wings?'

'Yes, that's him,' said Scarecrow. 'From what the

34

whale said we felt sure that this must be where he lives.'

'Dear, dear, dear,' said the professor in a voice of great distress. 'He should never have come back here. Oh dear me, no. As a matter of fact it was I myself who arranged for him to be taken away. I found a most respectable pig to adopt him; it was the only thing I could think of. Of course, the poor little creature would have felt homesick at first, but he was so very young that I had hoped he would soon get over it.'

'But what is the matter?' asked Scarecrow, puzzled. 'Is there anything wrong?'

'I fear there is a great deal wrong,' sighed the professor, 'a very great deal. Now he is back we shall have to consider what to do about it. I very much fear that you and your nice little friend will also be in danger. We shall have to see if we cannot get you all off the island before evening draws in, otherwise I am very much afraid that it might be too late.'

Mumfie tapped on the door politely and came in with Pinkey under one arm. Pinkey's nose was a good deal covered with stew. Mumfie had found him sitting in the ladle busily eating round himself.

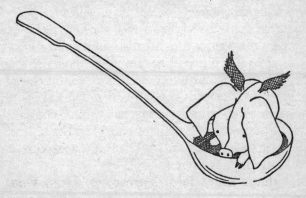

At the sight of the professor Pinkey gave a little squeal of delight. He fluttered across the room and perched on his shoulder.

'Look, he remembers me,' cried the old man delightedly. 'How very remarkable. I had hardly thought that he would, he was so very young when I sent him away. But dear me, you must all be hungry after your long journey. We will go into the kitchen and see what we can find, and then whilst you eat I had better explain the situation such as it is.'

He led the way towards the kitchen and absent-mindedly began to take down plates and bowls from the dresser. Scarecrow stirred the stew hopefully whilst Mumfie ran round helping to lay the table.

They sat round eating contentedly whilst the professor, between puffs at a long curling pipe, began to tell them a very strange story indeed.

CHAPTER FIVE

'WELL,' said the professor, 'I shall have to begin at the beginning, though, dear me, I must not take too long over my tale, because in some way I must manage to get you all safely off the island before dark. This used to be a most delightful island, harmonious, happy, and prosperous, set in mid-ocean as it is, with no outside influences to bother us here. But one evening a terrible calamity overtook us. It happened that I was sitting in my study perfecting a new magic upon which I had been working for some weeks, when I became aware of an odd rustling sound outside – a strange unfamiliar sound that made me go to the window to see what could be disturbing me at this hour.

'I saw an odd figure approaching through the trees. A stranger who seemed in some extraordinary way to come floating down the path as though he were not walking, but either was, or had just been, flying. He was enveloped from head to foot in a hooded cloak of dark material which gave him the appearance of some great bat or other creature of the night.

'I imagined that this person must have lost his way, but to my considerable surprise, and I will admit annoyance, he came on up to my door and knocked upon it. Courtesy made it impossible for me to pretend that I was out, as I feared that I must have been seen looking through the window. If only I had known the identity of my strange visitor I should have drawn the bolts and shut all the windows; anything to keep him away. I opened the door, and he glided past me into my study, where he sat down in the chair at my desk. All this time he had not said one word. He slipped back the hood and regarded me from dark eyes that burned and glittered, the only colour in his waxen face. I cannot describe to you how quiet all his movements were, so that when at last he spoke the harsh grating voice

came as a shock. I was filled with an unaccountable feeling of uneasiness.

' "Professor," he said, "my mistress has run out of Dreams." I assure you I was quite at a loss. I considered it a very strange remark, and did not know in what manner to reply to it. He evidently required some reply, for he looked at me expectantly.

' "That is indeed unfortunate," I said at last, "but I do not see in what way I can be of assistance to you."

' "That is what I have come here to tell you," said the stranger. "I believe that in these parts you have a very considerable reputation as a magician. I have been watching this island for many nights and I have decided that it will be very suitable to my purpose. Yes," he went on as though he had forgotten me, "the dark woods shall house my workshops, and the tree goblins shall work for me." He turned towards me as if suddenly aware of my presence again. "I am going to use this island for my dreams," he said. "And you, Professor, with your wisdom shall make a magic that will turn all the People, and Animals, and Things who live here into Dreams. In the day they will live here as ordinary people, but at night go out into the world to all those who sleep. The stories and patterns of the dreams will be woven in my workshops, but the dream spell must come from you, my dear Professor."

'As he finished speaking he smiled in a most unpleasant manner, and I looked at him with considerable indignation. I drew myself up and answered him with some heat.

' "Sir, much as I regret to disoblige you, I am afraid your suggestion is quite impossible. I can under no consideration consent to use my magic to such an intolerable purpose."

'I went on to tell him that the inhabitants of the
island would certainly be most unwilling to be turned
into dreams, and that he would do well to abandon all
idea of using this island for his plans. But he interrupted me with the same horrid laugh. "Professor, I

40

fear that you have no alternative." As he said this the strangest feeling stole over me. My head began to swim, and my knees to shake. The room swam before my eyes. I clutched at the table for support, and it was some moments before I was able to speak. Gradually my vision cleared, and I saw him again before me, clutching a small horn cup in his waxen hand.

' "Drink this," he ordered, holding it out to me. Faint as I was I took the cup from him and drank it down. Instantly I felt better, but in some extraordinary way my mind had changed. I no longer felt opposed to his plans, but listened in a docile manner whilst he instructed me to do his will.

'Blindly I went through my books, and when at last the fell magic was made, blindly I followed him out through the forest and on to the high hill that towers above the island. And there I stretched out my arms over the sleeping land, and said the words that would change all the happy people into sad Dreams. As soon as the words were spoken, darkness descended over the land like a cloak, and I remembered no more until in the morning I awoke, to find myself lying cramped and stiff beneath a thorn bush on the windy hill.'

'Oh, but how dreadful!' said Mumfie, who had been listening wide-eyed to the professor's story. 'What a horrid person; he must have bewitched you. But who was he? You didn't say who he was.'

'He was the Secretary,' said the professor, and drew his hand across his eyes rather wearily. 'The terrible Secretary of Night.'

'But, sir?' Scarecrow sounded rather perplexed. 'Couldn't you have made another spell when he had gone, to change the people all back again?'

'Unhappily no,' sighed the professor. 'For when I

41

had pronounced the spell he took my magic box away from me; little magics I can still make, but the power of great magic is gone from me, and I do not know where it is hidden.'

'Oh dear, oh dear,' said Mumfie, thinking that the professor looked sad. 'If only you could find it again, then you could make another undoing sort of magic, and everything would be all right again. But you still haven't explained about Pinkey, sir.'

'No, no indeed,' began the professor. He looked round for Pinkey who was curled up on a chair. He had over-eaten, and was now busily sleeping it off.

'My, how that pig does sleep,' muttered Scarecrow. 'I think there's someone at the door, sir.'

'Someone at the door? Good gracious me, I think you must be mistaken. Nobody comes to see me these days. Why, you are the first visitors I have had for months.'

The professor got up and went over to the window to look out. He gave a little gasp of surprise.

'Bless my soul, this is most peculiar. This is more than peculiar.'

'What?' asked Mumfie, climbing on to the window-sill to look. 'What's peculiar, please? Why, that's a goblin,' he said, surprised. 'I know that's a goblin 'cos I knows what they looks like. Shall I go and answer the door for you, sir?' he asked hopefully.

The professor called out to detain him, but he trotted happily out of the room and opened the front door. There on the doorstep was a funny little fellow with very short legs and very red cheeks, and a bright blue jerkin. On seeing Mumfie his eyes opened wide with surprise.

'Oh, goodness, I didn't know the old buffer had

42

visitors. I'll come back another time.' He turned, and surprisingly fast on his fat little legs streaked down the path again.

But Mumfie rushed after him, determined not to lose his first goblin so soon. He had to chase him quite a long way into the wood, but at last managed to catch up with him.

'Wait a minute,' he puffed, a good deal out of breath. 'What did you want to run away for? You should have come in and seen the professor; he was just saying that he hardly ever had any visitors. He must be quite lonely.'

The goblin looked at him rather strangely.

'That's true enough,' he said. 'But I'm the sort of visitor that he'd be likely to resent. It was only as a very last resort that I came to him at all. I certainly didn't expect to find anyone with him. However, since you were, we might as well pass the time of day. Have a sandwich?'

He fished in his pocket and pulled out a neat paper packet of sandwiches. From the other pocket he drew out a bottle of ginger-beer. He pushed in the glass ball stopper with a very broad thumb, took a drink, and handed the bottle to Mumfie.

'Thank you very much,' said Mumfie, feeling the ginger-beer bubbling pleasantly inside. 'This is very odd, I thought you weren't supposed to be friends of the professor's.'

'Oh we don't object to him at all. Not us young ones. We just aren't allowed to have anything to do with him, that's all. I should get into trouble if anyone had seen me today. As it is I ought not to be sitting about here talking to you.' He glanced round nervously.

'What did you want to see him about?' asked Mumfie curiously.

'Well, I'm in a bad fix. Look, I really shouldn't tell you, but I can't help liking the look of you. Promise not to repeat it if I tell you; you don't live here, do you? Or are you by any chance one of the new ones that somebody's thought up?'

'No, I'm not a new anything,' said Mumfie excitedly. 'Do tell me, I won't tell anyone – least not anyone but Scarecrow. He's my friend, and we haven't got any secrets. But you can trust him absolutely.'

'Well, it would be rather a relief to tell somebody. Do you mind coming inside the tree though, I think it would be safer than out here.'

He got up and scratched at the tree-trunk. To Mumfie's amazement there was a creaking sound and a little door opened. The goblin went inside, beckoning Mumfie to follow him.

'Take care how you go,' he whispered, 'and don't fall down the steps.'

Mumfie went in after him, and no sooner was he inside than a gust of wind blew through the forest and slammed the door to behind him.

CHAPTER SIX

'OH my,' said Mumfie, 'it's dark in here. I can't see where I am.'

'Take hold of my hand. There, we'll sit down on the steps. Now, you see, the trouble is this. I was helping old Waxy make one of the patterns for the dreams when he was called off on business. He left me to finish it and take it to the main office when it was done because it was wanted for tonight. Well, on my way to the main office I fell in with some of my friends who were playing Push and Grab in the passage, so I joined in the game. It's rather a scrambly sort of game – perhaps you know it. Well, anyway, after a little while I remembered about the pattern. It was getting late, so I thought I'd better take it in – I felt about for it, and

very nearly had a fit because I couldn't find it anywhere. At first I thought one of my friends must have
picked it up and hidden it as a joke, but they knew no
more about it than I did.

'Of course Waxy got into trouble for not having his
pattern in on time, and *I* got into trouble from Waxy.
Terrible trouble, I assure you. I'm still sore. I've been
searching about all over the place this morning and still
can't find it, and you see if I don't find it by tonight
then I'll be put on to doing nightmares for a whole
fortnight, and the thought of that is more than I can
stand. So in desperation I suddenly thought of the
professor and wondered if he could possibly help me
with a finding magic. He's awfully clever, you know.'

Mumfie was just go-
ing to say that the pro-
fessor could no longer
make any magics, when
something warned him
not to mention it. His
eyes were becoming ac-
customed to the gloom,
and he could just make
out the steps leading
down steeply under
their feet.

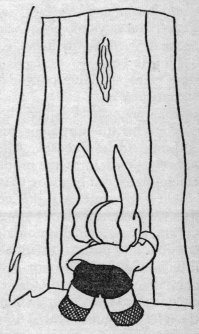

'What's down there?'
he was beginning, when
there was a creaking
sound below them.

The goblin started.
'Sh,' he whispered.
'There's someone com-
ing up the stairs.

47

Quick, you must get out of here. It would never do for you to be found here. Awfully nice to have known you.'

He rushed to the door and pushed it, but the wind had slammed it to with such force that it had jammed. He pushed it frantically, but could not budge it. The steps were coming nearer, Mumfie sprang up in a fright as an old man came hobbling up, peering about him through the darkness.

'Who is there?' he called in a cracked voice. He almost bumped into the scared Mumfie before he saw him. He grabbed him by the wrist and stared into his face.

'It's all right, sir,' said the small goblin in a shaking voice. 'Just a friend of mine, sir. We were only sitting on the top step, sir.'

'A friend of yours, eh?' the old man snapped. 'Very peculiar friends you have. And who gave you permission to bring your friends inside, may I ask? And what were *you* doing outside? You're supposed to be on duty.'

'I'm sorry, sir,' snuffled the goblin. 'I just popped out for a breath of fresh air, sir.'

'Don't make excuses, Alfie,' said the old man severely. 'Well, since he's inside, he'd better stay inside. He might as well be made use of.'

'Oh NO!' squeaked the goblin, 'he's just going. You're going now, aren't you?'

'Yes, I am,' said Mumfie decidedly. He rushed for the door and pushed it with all his might. It opened a little way and he was just pushing through when the old goblin caught hold of him and grabbed him back. As he pulled, the door swung to again, catching the corner of Mumfie's coat. There was a tearing sound as

48

the goblin wrenched. He let go, and Mumfie sat down with a flop.

'Oh!' he said with dismay. 'You've torn my coat, you horrid rude old man. My beautiful red coat. Selina will be very angry.' He was so distressed that he nearly burst into tears. But the old man jerked him to his feet and began hurrying him down the steep steps.

'Now, you, back to your workshop,' he ordered Alfie. 'I'll have something to say to you later.'

'Oh, please don't go, don't leave me,' wailed Mumfie, by this time thoroughly frightened.

'He'll do as he is told,' snapped the goblin. 'And double quick time too. Now be off with you!'

Alfie brushed past Mumfie as he walked away.

'Cheer up,' he managed to whisper, 'I'll come and find you.' He went off down a long winding passage.

The way was dimly lit with paper lanterns. The old man pushed Mumfie along.

'Pick up your feet and march smartly,' he ordered. 'We don't hold with shuffling here.'

'Where are you taking me?' asked Mumfie.

'Don't chatter,' snapped the goblin. 'Hurry along and keep to the left. Can't you read the signs?'

Mumfie looked up to see that there were notices along the passage saying, KEEP TO THE LEFT. They were rounding a corner when he nearly collided with another goblin coming towards them at a great pace.

'Oh, Waxy,' he puffed, 'I've been looking for you everywhere. The boss wants you in room 21 about that pattern of yours.' He stared at Mumfie curiously. 'That's a new one you've got, isn't it? I haven't seen that one before, have I?'

'You have not,' said Waxy. 'Mind your own business. Tell the boss I'll be along presently. Come along, come along. Don't stand there gaping.'

He pushed Mumfie forward. Mumfie turned round to see the goblin staring after them as they rounded the corner. They came out into a strange circular hall with doors leading from it, and went over to a door marked

DREAMS

(In)

The goblin opened it, and pushed Mumfie into a room furnished as an office, in which was a clerk sitting at a desk. He looked up smartly and tucked his pen behind his ear.

'Hold this one for now,' ordered Waxy, 'I'll be back presently.'

'Dream or Nightmare?' asked the clerk, pulling out a large ledger.

'Don't know,' said Waxy. 'Nightmare, I should

imagine. Hold him for query. I'll be back.' He went out of the room slamming the door behind him.

'Now that's awkward,' muttered the clerk. 'I do wish they'd be more specific.'

'I beg your pardon?' said Mumfie, who did not know what 'specific' meant.

'Not at all,' said the clerk. 'It's not your fault, it's just a question of the inks.'

Mumfie noticed that along his desk were many bottles of different coloured inks.

'You see, if you're a Dream you go down in red or green according to your classification, but if you're a Nightmare you are entered in blue or purple depending on the strength. I think I'd better enter you up later. I'll just take your name for now.'

'Mumfie,' said Mumfie shyly. 'But please I'd much rather go home.'

'That's what they all say at first,' said the clerk, 'but never mind, it's not so bad once you get used to it. That is, if you're in the dream section. I'll try and get you in there if I can. Anyway, you'll have plenty of people to talk to. Come along, I've got a lot of work to do so I can't stay here talking.'

He pushed back a low swing door that came up to the level of his desk and crossed an empty hall, round which were hung a great many peculiar and rather exciting pictures. Mumfie would have liked to stay and look at some of them, but the clerk hurried him forward. 'Come along, in here, please. You can see those another time – though they're not worth looking at,' he added. 'People's dreams are best kept in the head and not put down on paper, in MY opinion. But no doubt I'm old-fashioned.'

He opened a small green door at the end of the room

51

by the rather peculiar method of stooping down and blowing through the key-hole. The door swung open with a little pop, and Mumfie found himself in a great chamber with a domed roof. He heard the clerk go out and the door shut behind him.

He looked around him, feeling rather lost and lonely. He did not at first notice that there were a great many people in the vast room. They were sitting or standing about in groups and took no notice of him at all. He walked over to a group of people rather shyly, and saw with surprise that they were bending over a great jig-saw puzzle, half completed, that was laid out on the table before them. They were all trying to finish it, but it looked very large and difficult.

'Oo,' said Mumfie, 'may I help? I loves jig-saws.'

There was a movement in the group, several people turning round to stare at him.

But Mumfie was looking with amazement at a large pink pig standing the other side of the table. He looked round the room, and was surprised to see People, Animals, and Things, all clustered together in the most extraordinary way. A Loaf of Bread waddled across and took its place beside him. It regarded him solemnly through currant eyes.

'Bad luck, old man, bad luck,' it wheezed. 'Which puzzle are you on?'

'I don't know,' answered Mumfie, bewildered. 'I wasn't told anything about it.'

'Ain't got his instructions,' said the Loaf to the room in general. 'Now isn't that a shame. Well, it's to be hoped you're not on *that* one.' He pointed to a table in a far corner of the room, round which a number of creatures were peeping fearfully. They handled the

puzzle pieces with reluctance and did not seem to be enjoying themselves at all.

'Oh dear, oh dear,' sighed Mumfie. 'What is happening? I feel just as though I were dreaming.'

'Yes, I know,' said the Loaf. 'We all feels like that at first. You'll settle down. In fact you may even get to like it. You may find yourself quite popular like me. People likes dreaming about food, they do – not that I'm as popular as some of the fancy foods. See old Toffee over there; he's got so many people dreaming about him that he's quite swollen-headed, and you should see the airs Miss Milk Bread gives herself, she'll hardly speak to me just because I'm only a Cottage Loaf. But I mustn't keep you; time I got back to my puzzle or I shall never find out where I fit in before it's time to go off tonight. So long.'

It waved in a friendly way, and waddled back to its own table.

Mumfie's eyes travelled back to the large pig, who had evidently just found her piece, for she put it in with a grunt and trotted away from the table towards a long plush-covered sofa on to which she flopped, and lay down. Mumfie followed her, staring hard. A feeling of hope and excitement came over him, for on her back, just behind the ears, were tucked a neat little pair of pink wings.

CHAPTER SEVEN

MUMFIE came over to the sofa and scrambled on to it. 'Excuse me, madam,' he began, 'but have you by any chance a relative called Pinkey?'

The old pig sat bolt upright. 'What did you say?' she asked, excitement growing in her face.

'A pig called Pinkey. He's very small but there's a quite remarkable likeness; he has wings too, only his are blue. So I wondered.'

'Well my gracious! I have a son called Pinkey; my youngest. Of course his wings are blue. Blue for a boy and pink for a girl. But no, it can't be the same. The poor dear professor had him sent away from the island when all this trouble began. It must be someone else.' She sank down again with a grunt of disappointment.

'Oh, but I believe it is!' said Mumfie excitedly. 'You see we don't live here, we only arrived this morning and we brought Pinkey with us. He wasn't happy with the pig family he lived with, 'cos you see they hadn't got any wings and they used to tease him about his flying. He was so lonely and miserable that we decided to help him find his real family. He's with the professor now, only the professor is very worried about him and says we ought to leave the island before night time. I couldn't quite make out why.'

He paused for breath, but the old pig had got up again and was wuffling her nose in the air with excitement.

'Oh, how kind of you,' she said. 'But oh dear, oh dear, he should never have come back. Of course he was far too small when the professor sent him away to know anything about it. You see, in the happy days before all the trouble we used to be the professor's pigs. Very kind to us he was, and quite devoted to the children. I always thought that he took to them so much because after his little granddaughter disappeared he had no young things about the house. Pinkey was his especial pet ever since he was a baby. Used to follow him around wherever he went. Fair pretty to see it was. Although we assured him it wasn't his fault, the poor professor was so grieved at bringing misfortune upon us that he was quite broken up. But he was determined that they shouldn't have Pinkey. He simply couldn't imagine Pinkey as anyone's nightmare. So he came down to the sty and suggested that he should smuggle him off the island before it was too late. He said he could manage to get him adopted by a pig family that lived a long way off. It was a terrible wrench parting with him to be sure, and him my youngest, but it seemed the best thing to do for him. I've always tried to consider their futures, and seeing that the old gentleman was so kind it seemed selfish to stand in his way. Besides, the professor had never given up hope of putting things right one day, and then he would have been able to come home again. Oh dear!' she sighed heavily. 'If only the poor old man could discover where they had hidden his magic. But what are you doing down here, my dear. Surely it is very dangerous?'

'Oh dear, I hope not,' said Mumfie unhappily. 'You see I was talking in the forest to a nice little goblin, and a horrid old man came up and caught us, and he sent me down here. Scarecrow will be wondering whatever has happened to me. My goodness, and he may come and try to find me and then they'll capture him too. But I would like to try one of those puzzles.'

The great hall was beginning to get quite dark and gloomy. People were leaving the tables and lining up in long rows, two by two facing towards the entrance.

'Oh well,' sighed the pig, 'time to be going.'

'Where are you going?' asked Mumfie, sad at the thought of losing his new friend. 'Couldn't I come too?'

'Good gracious, no,' said the old lady. 'You try and hide, my dear. We are all going out to act our dreams. We shan't be back until morning. I don't know however I shall get through my part tonight, what with my lumbago and all.' She sighed again, thinking wistfully of her cosy sty at the end of the professor's orchard. She wished that she could lie down for a nice sleep with her children all scampering around her, and the comfortable noise of old Joe her husband wortling about in the forest for acorns. Then she remembered the small elephant, who was looking at her hopefully.

'You'd better hide, my dear. They seem to have forgotten you. Get behind that sofa before the goblins come in to fetch us. Then perhaps you will be able to slip out later when it gets dark. Quick, I hear them coming.'

Mumfie made haste to take her advice. He rushed over to the sofa and crouched behind it as the door blew open admitting two old goblins.

They marshalled all the People and Animals and Things out of the doors in a long silent stream. It seemed a long time when the last couples had filed through and the door was shut behind them. Mumfie was alone in the dark empty hall. He clutched on to the sofa, feeling very frightened.

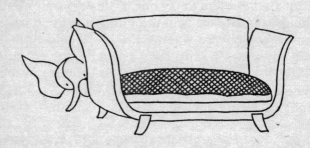

'Oh, Scarecrow,' he whispered to himself. 'I do wish you was here.' As he crouched in the darkness he felt himself growing more and more frightened every minute. He almost began to wish that the bad-tempered Waxy would come back for him. Anything would be better than being shut up here in the dark.

'Now, Mumfie, pull yourself together,' he said to himself severely. He suddenly had an idea. He crept out from behind the sofa and went over to the door.

He had remembered how the clerk opened it by blowing through the key-hole. He stole over to it, and reaching up blew hard. To his disappointment nothing happened. He blew again harder still until he felt as though his cheeks would burst, then he sat down on the floor to think. No, of course that was wrong because the door opened into the room towards him. Perhaps if he SUCKED in his breath very hard near the key-hole he could manage it that way.

He stood on tip-toe with his mouth close to the key-hole and sucked as hard as he possibly could. The door flew open with a little plop, knocking him over backwards.

'My!' said Mumfie, picking himself up and dusting himself. 'I didn't expect that.'

He peeped through the doorway wondering what he should say to the clerk, but to his excitement he saw that the outer room was empty. He rushed across it, but alas, the door was locked and no amount of puffing and blowing would open it.

'Well, that's that,' said Mumfie bravely, though he could have cried with disappointment. 'I suppose I shall just have to wait until somebody comes for me. Anyway, it's nicer in here, at least there's some light.'

He went over to the desk and sat down on the clerk's stool. Presently he got tired of having nothing to do so he began to play with the bottles of coloured inks. He was so happily engaged in squashing out some very good coloured butterflies, that he did not hear the door open.

'Oh, goodness,' said a familiar voice, 'I never expected to find you here. Whatever are you doing?'

Mumfie looked up to see Alfie, who had crept quietly into the room.

'I couldn't get out, and there wasn't anything to do, so I thought I'd just make a few butterflies until somebody came in.'

Alfie looked at the butterflies and thought them very fine indeed. He wanted to try some himself, but it really was not safe to hang about.

'Come along,' he said. 'There's hardly anyone about now and I might be able to get you safely out.'

They stole out of the room and along the dimly lit passage.

'Did you find your pattern?' whispered Mumfie.

'No I didn't,' answered Alfie sadly. 'I got into terrible trouble, and now I've been put on to piecing together the nightmares for the next week, unless I can find it by nine o'clock. It's eight now, and I've looked simply everywhere.'

'Well, p'r'aps if we looked together we might find it,' suggested Mumfie helpfully. 'I always think it's a good plan to look in all the most unlikely places. For instance I suppose you've searched in all your pockets?'

'Why of course,' said Alfie. 'I turned them all inside out. I even looked inside my stockings and in the soles of my shoes, though what I should have put it in there for I don't know.'

'Oh, you might have. Scarecrow often puts brown paper in his boots, he says it keeps his feet warm in the cold weather. I suppose you did look inside your hat?'

Alfie looked at him in a rather dazed manner, and took his hat off his head. There was a crackling sound and a folded piece of stiff paper fell out of it to the ground. They both dived for it.

'Well, I never!' said Alfie, holding it out as though he could not believe his eyes. He started to jump around with excitement.

'That's it all right. Fancy my never thinking of looking in my hat! Oh how lovely, now I shan't have to do the nightmares. You are kind. Here, I shall give you one of my sweets for that.'

He fished in his pocket and held out a pointed paper bag of toffee.

'Thank you,' said Mumfie, taking two. 'Thank you very much indeed. I really was getting rather hungry, I think it must be long past my usual supper time. Eight o'clock, did you say? Oh dear, oh dear, Scarecrow will be in a terrible state wondering what's happened to me. I really think I'd better be going if you don't mind.'

'I do mind. I mind very much,' said Alfie sadly, as they hurried down the passage. 'I shall miss you.'

They were just rounding a bend, when to their dismay they heard footsteps coming along behind them.

'Oh mercy,' squeaked Mumfie, 'there's somebody coming.'

Alfie glanced behind him and then seized Mumfie by the arm. He pulled open a door on the right and dragged him inside. 'Quick, in here.' He closed it behind them just as voices sounded loudly outside.

They crouched down behind the door. It seemed that they were in a small cupboard. People were talking outside. 'Oh dear,' whispered Alfie, 'that's Waxy's voice I'm sure. I do wish they'd go on.'

'Humph!' said the voice. 'Who has been leaving toffee paper about in the passages I should like to know?

Get a broom, Edward, and clear it up. I cannot abide such untidiness.'

To their dismay they saw the handle turning and the door of the cupboard began to open. Mumfie seized hold of it and tugged for dear life but the person called Edward was evidently stronger than he.

'It appears to be stuck,' they heard him say. Then he gave a tremendous heave, so that the door burst open suddenly, flinging Mumfie into the passage. Alfie tumbled out behind him.

They looked up to see Waxy regarding them with a baleful eye. 'What is the meaning of this?' he thundered. 'What are you doing out here. Why haven't you gone off with the others. I put you in the puzzle room.'

'Nobody told me what to do,' said Mumfie stoutly. 'They all went out and left me alone in there, and I don't like being all by myself in such a big room, and so I came out to see if I could find anyone. Then I bumped into Alfie.'

'Silence!' barked the old Goblin, 'hold your tongue. And get up off the floor, I don't know what you're sitting about for.' He turned to the two goblins who were standing behind him.

'Take them along to the cells, they had better be held there until we can find out what to do with them.'

'Oh NO!' wailed Alfie. 'We don't want to go there. Please, Waxy. We won't be naughty again, honestly we won't, only please don't send us there.'

Mumfie on seeing his little friend's distress became most indignant. 'You can't put me in a cell,' he bellowed, 'nor him either. I won't go. I'm a free subject, and you can't lock me up in your old prison. If you do, Scarecrow will be terribly angry and he'll come and blow you all up.' He was quite red in the face with indignation.

But the two goblins seized hold of him and the protesting Alfie and began dragging them along the passage. Mumfie fought lustily but it was no use; his goblin was remarkably strong. They were pulled along until they came to an iron door. The goblin hammered on it, and it was opened from inside by an immense green toad.

'Here's two prisoners for you, Jimmy,' he said. 'Put them in the refractory cell and hold them there until further orders. You had better handcuff them together, they're giving a lot of trouble. Especially THAT one.' He glared at Mumfie, who glared back in the most ferocious manner possible. The goblin went out muttering indignantly to himself.

'Well,' croaked the toad, 'come along, and look sharp about it. And in case you don't feel like 'urrying, take a look at this.'

It drew a large truncheon from its belt and brandished it threateningly. It drove them down a narrow passage, on either side of which were cells with steel bars across them. It unlocked a door and pushed them inside, and when they were safely locked in, waddled away down the passage.

'He's forgotten about the handcuffs,' whispered Mumfie. 'That's one good thing. And at least he's put us both in the same cell. I was so afraid that we'd be separated.'

But poor Alfie was so dejected that he refused to be comforted. He sat down on the hard wooden bed and a tear rolled down his cheek.

'Never mind,' comforted Mumfie, sitting down beside him, but he was feeling very dispirited himself, and

not a little frightened. 'Scarecrow will come and rescue us. He's wonderfully clever, Scarecrow is. He will be sure to come and look for me.' He stared hopefully through the close iron bars.

CHAPTER EIGHT

'WHATEVER is Mumfie doing?' said Scarecrow.
'He's been a tremendous long time at the door.
Excuse me, sir, but I think I'd better go and
see.'

He went out to the front door, but to his surprise
there was no sign either of Mumfie or the goblin.

'Mumfie,' he called out, 'where are you?'

He went round the house to see if they had gone
round to the back, but it was quiet and deserted.

'Gracious,' said Scarecrow, beginning to be alarmed.
'Where on earth can he have got to?' He went out into
the clearing and bellowed, 'MUMFIE!' at the top of his

voice. The call went up into the forest and was lost in the swaying branches, but there was no answer.

'Oh my goodness!' cried Scarecrow, now seriously alarmed. He ran back into the cottage and burst into the professor's study.

'Oh, sir,' he said, 'I can't see any sign of them.'

The professor was most distressed, but quite unable to suggest any reasonable place where they might have gone. Pinkey had gone to sleep again, so they put him down in the armchair, and went out into the forest to search.

They wandered about all day, until at last the old man became so weary that he had to sit down.

'You go back sir,' suggested Scarecrow kindly. 'You look quite worn out. I can get along quicker by myself, and I'll come and tell you as soon as I have any news.'

'Well, I think I had better go back. After all, he may return to the cottage and wonder where we have gone. I will blow my whistle if he comes and then you will hear me wherever you are, and be able to find your way back by the sound. But I beg you to be careful and not stray too far. It would not do any good for you both to get lost, and whatever happens you must return to the cottage before nightfall.'

'All right, sir, I will,' Scarecrow promised.

He watched the old man slowly wending his way through the trees, leaning heavily upon his stick. He waved until he was out of sight, and then returned once more to his search.

He was so worried that he hardly knew what to do; he began running through the trees, calling Mumfie's name. His coat caught in the brambles and became more and more tattered. His legs ached and his head ached, and he noticed with dismay that it was begin-

ning to grow dark. He did not like being out in the forest after dark and the professor had particularly told him to go back, but whatever was he to do.

'Oh, I can't go back and leave him,' he sobbed. 'Oh, Mumfie, wherever have you got to? Oh dear, oh dear.' He sat down under a tree and tried to pull himself together and think what he should do next. He fished in his pocket for a hankie and blew his nose. He was staring in front of him when suddenly he noticed something red caught in the trunk of a tree opposite. He got up and went over to it. It was a small piece of red cloth that seemed to be wedged into the bark. Scarecrow leant down to look at it closer. It was now so dark that it was quite difficult to see.

'My goodness!' he said excitedly. 'That's a bit of

Mumfie's coat, that is. But how did it get caught on here? It isn't caught, it's wedged – almost as though there were a crack in the tree-trunk. I wonder if it *is* a crack or if by any chance it's a door.'

He remembered the professor saying that goblins lived in the woods. In that case it was quite likely that there were entrances to their houses through the tree-trunks. He began to tap at the bark, hoping to find a spring. He tapped and scratched and pushed, but nothing happened. He scratched his head in a puzzled manner, and was just going to try again, when he thought he heard sounds coming from inside the tree. It was now quite dark in the forest. The noises were sounding louder; an endless shuffling as though many people were approaching.

'My word!' said Scarecrow to himself. 'If they're coming out I had better hide, then perhaps I can slip through the doorway after them.'

He had just time to scuttle behind one of the tree's big roots when the door swung slowly open, and a strange procession emerged.

Scarecrow watched them in wide-eyed amazement. An endless stream of People, Animals and Things, with two goblins marshalling them along. They walked in a dreamlike manner, but to Scarecrow's astonishment those at the head of the column began to lift into the air. They seemed to float rather than fly up into the tree-tops, soon to be lost in the darkness.

Scarecrow looked towards the door; now he would have to take a chance. He pulled his hat far down over his eyes, turned up his coat collar, and sidled slowly round the tree-trunk.

The goblins were watching the last of their charges waft up into the air.

'Well, that's *them* off for the night,' muttered one of them. 'Coming round to the Pig and Acorn, Stumper?' He turned to his companion, who was busy packing a large pipe.

'Well, I don't mind if I do,' replied Stumper. 'I've got a thirst I wouldn't sell for sixpence halfpenny.'

Scarecrow did not wait to hear the rest of the conversation; all this time he had been edging his way nearer and nearer to the open door. He had just managed to slip inside when it was pushed to and closed with a bang.

It was so dark inside that at first he could not see where he was. He felt in his pocket for the matches, but when he tried to strike one, found that they were still damp. He felt the ground with his feet, and it was a good thing that he did so, otherwise he might have fallen headlong down the steps.

'Huh! seems to be stairs,' he muttered to himself. 'I wish to goodness the matches hadn't got wet.' He went carefully down the stairs, feeling against the wall to guide himself.

At the foot of the stairs it became lighter, and he found himself in the passage. He whispered Mumfie's name, hoping that he might be hiding somewhere near, but dared not call out too loud in case some unfriendly person should hear him. Nobody seemed to be about, and so he went right along the passage until he came to the round hall. He looked at all the doors, wondering which he should try.

'Wonder what I'd better pretend I'm doing if I bump into someone?' he thought. He noticed the door marked 'Dreams,' of course the professor had told them that the goblins made dreams underneath the woods. He thought of the long procession he had seen outside, floating up into the air. 'I suppose those were the Dreams coming out. P'r'aps I'd better pretend I'm a dream, though if that were the case I should have been with the others. Never mind, I'll be a new dream someone has made up, and I'll have lost my way or something. I'll think of something when the time comes; best not to make too many plans ahead.

'I'll try this door for a start, no good trying the Dream door as they've all gone out. But it will do to mark my place with if I'm wrong the first time.' He took the door on the left, opened it quietly and poked his head inside.

He was quite amazed to find himself in a garden. It was quite unlike any garden that he had ever seen, because it was all dark blue. He thought at first that it must be the evening light, but when he walked amongst the trees and flowers he saw that they were indeed blue, even the grass was a sapphire carpet under his feet.

'Oh my!' he said, 'I wonder if Mumfie has come in here. If he has he must be quite enjoying himself. What a strange place. The only thing against it is that it's a bit cold. In fact, it's distinctly cold.' He pulled his coat closer about him, and stuffed his hands into his pockets to keep them warm.

Banks of flowers grew amongst the trees, they smelt lovely and he stooped to pick one and put it in his buttonhole. He was so intent on this that he was exceedingly startled when he realized that there was someone standing quite close to him. This person was surrounded by a strange soft light that gave off a pleasant warmth. Scarecrow looked through the light to see a rather fat baby in a short blue frock.

'My goodness!' he said, 'but you quite startled me.

Wherever did you spring from? I didn't hear you coming.'

'I'm sorry,' said the child, 'I didn't mean to startle you. I don't come FROM anywhere. I live here.'

'You're very bright,' said Scarecrow, 'AND warm, which is a good thing for you. It's cold down here.'

'Of course I'm bright,' answered the child. 'I'm a Night-light. Only I'm not needed tonight, so I can play in the garden. We're playing hide-and-seek now, only I'm He and they haven't called yet.'

'Are there many of you?' Scarecrow asked. He was hoping that one of them might have seen Mumfie.

'Oh yes, quite a lot; in fact, very few of us were needed this evening.'

'I suppose you haven't seen any other strangers about tonight?' asked Scarecrow hopefully.

The child shook its head, and was about to reply when a long Coo-eeee sang through the garden.

'Oh, they're ready, I must go.' The bright light danced away through the flowers and was lost among some shining blue bushes. Scarecrow heard pattering feet and peals of laughter. He wished that he could join in the game, but he was no nearer to finding Mumfie. He went on through the garden looking about amongst the trees. Occasionally he caught sight of one of the bright children running about, but they were all too engrossed in their game to stop and talk to him.

'Perhaps I had better go back and try another door,' he thought. He retraced his steps, only to find to his dismay that he had not the slightest idea where he was. Everything looked alike. He tried to find his own foot-prints, but they made no impression at all in the stiff dry grass. He wandered about for a long time; but it was no use, he was quite lost. He sat down to think

things out, the only thing to do was to find one of the children and get it to show him the way out. He called out several times, but they all seemed to have disappeared. He could have cried with agitation. This was a silly situation – Mumfie lost, and now he had gone and got himself lost as well. That was very helpful, that was. He was a fine fellow and no mistake. He was wondering whatever to do next when he became aware that somebody was walking in the garden. For no reason at all he suddenly became excited and a little awed. He looked up from under his hat-brim to see a very lovely lady in a pale dress, with a veil over her hair, coming through the trees towards him. She walked beautifully so that she seemed to be treading on air. The flowers swayed towards her, tangling her skirts. She had been picking them, for she held a bunch of moonflowers in her hand.

Though she was looking straight in his direction she did not appear to have seen him. Scarecrow decided that he had better hide. He crept behind a tree and waited breathlessly. She did not turn her head, but called to him to come out. Her voice was little more than a whisper, but it was a voice you could not disobey.

Scarecrow came out from behind the tree and took off his hat politely.

'What are you doing in my garden?' asked the lady.

Scarecrow watched a dark ring that gleamed on her finger. He did not know what to say; he wanted to tell her the truth and ask her if she had seen Mumfie about, but she was so remote and beautiful that he felt a little afraid of her. He was such a long time in answering that he expected her to be angry with him, but she just stood quietly, waiting for him to speak. A soft breeze blew through the garden swaying the long flowers in her hand.

'I don't quite know,' stammered Scarecrow at last, his voice sounding very loud to him. 'I got in here by mistake.'

'Why are you not with the other Dreams?'

'Oh dear,' thought Scarecrow desperately, 'this is beginning to get a little difficult.' He made another effort. 'Well, you see, Ma'am, it's my night off,' he blurted out hopefully.

She looked at him and smiled in a way that he could not quite make out.

'Did the Secretary say that you might have an evening off?' she asked.

'Oh no,' said Scarecrow quickly. 'At least, I mean . . .'

'I see. Well, in that case you had better keep out of his way. You can do a little work in the garden if you like. Go along that path until you come to one of the tool-sheds. Get yourself a broom, and if anyone comes you can be sweeping up the leaves.'

'Yes, Ma'am, certainly, Ma'am,' answered Scarecrow happily, smiling at her. He was glad to be let off so lightly. He ran off down the path. When he had gone a little way he turned round to see the lady looking after him with a rather sad little smile on her face.

'I don't believe she's very happy,' he said to himself. 'And she doesn't seem to think very much of her Secretary; she even sounded a little afraid of him. Never mind, perhaps if I do a good job of this sweeping she may be pleased; and I can go on until I find the entrance.'

He had just found himself a broom in the tool-shed when he heard a strange croaking voice saying,

' 'Urry along there, 'urry along.'

He peeped from behind the door, to see an immense green toad shepherding two people through the garden. He drove them in front of him so that Scarecrow could not make them out very clearly. He was making up his mind to stay hidden until they were safely out of the way when he heard a familiar voice saying,

'Oh please, Jimmy, need we hurry so fast – this is such a lovely garden.'

Scarecrow's heart leapt with delight. He rushed out of the shed, waving the broom in his excitement, and began running after them. As he ran he was thinking fast. It was evident that the toad was driving them somewhere, and that he did not seem particularly friendly. Supposing they were prisoners? Then if he ran out and showed himself in all probability he would be captured too, and would be powerless to help them.

'I'll follow them quietly and see where they go,' he said to himself, slowing down. 'If Mumfie sees me he is sure to let out a squeak of surprise or something.' He was glad that he had brought the broom, for if the toad should turn round suddenly he could pretend to be a gardener. He followed them softly, dodging behind the trees and tall flowers.

They had not gone very far when Mumfie seemed suddenly to halt. He turned round, searching the garden expectantly. Scarecrow popped behind a tree, making frantic signs to Mumfie not to notice him.

'Now then, 'urry along there, 'urry along,' wheezed the toad. It turned round to see what Mumfie was looking at, but Scarecrow was again safely hidden behind a wide trunk.

'What were you staring at?' asked the toad suspiciously.

'Nuffin',' said Mumfie happily. 'I thought I saw a dickey bird, that's all.'

He poked the small goblin and marched along proudly in front of the gaoler.

'I knew Scarecrow would come,' he said to himself happily.

Scarecrow crept out from behind the tree, and followed the three cautiously.

CHAPTER NINE

MUMFIE trotted along beside the goblin, urging him
to go faster, so that the toad was hard put to it to keep
up with them.

' 'Ere!' it called after them. 'Not so fast there. Not
so fast.'

'But you told us to 'urry up,' called Mumfie. 'Come
on,' he whispered to the mystified Alfie. 'Hurry up, I
don't want it to hear what I'm saying.'

'I can't see what you're so excited about all of a
sudden,' grumbled Alfie.

'Cheer up!' Mumfie beamed at him. 'Everything's going to be all right now. Scarecrow's here; he's following behind.'

'Now then,' bellowed the toad, 'none of that whispering. What were you talking about?'

'I was saying what a becoming colour green was for toads,' said Mumfie naughtily.

'Becoming WHAT?' snapped the toad. 'Oh, becoming. I see what you mean.' It swelled out with pleasure, so that Mumfie guessed that it did not often receive compliments, and felt rather sorry for it.

'Why is this garden all blue, Jimmy?' he asked in a friendly voice.

'It's Night's garden,' replied the toad, as though that were explanation enough.

The garden was becoming more and more beautiful as they went along. They had come out into a clearing now, a long blue lawn with trees on either side. At the end of the lawn stood a cool palace. A pale radiance shone down through the trees, throwing long shadows from the slender pillars and down the long steps.

'Oo, my!' said Mumfie. 'Are we going in there?'

'Yes, you are,' said the toad. 'Though why he's sent for you himself I don't know. The goblins usually manage to deal with matters like you. I shouldn't like to be in *your* shoes,' it added darkly.

They had by now reached the steps. Mumfie looked anxiously round to see if Scarecrow were still following, but he was nowhere in sight.

'I expect he's waiting until we get inside,' he comforted himself.

The toad led them through a tall archway, and tapped twice on a door. He waited patiently for some minutes until the door slowly opened, bathing them in a clear pale light. Mumfie was surprised to see that it had apparently opened by itself.

'In you go,' said the toad. 'Wait here until somebody comes for you.'

'But aren't you coming in with us?' asked Mumfie. He did not like the idea of their being left in this strange palace all by themselves, and he was afraid that when the toad went away it might bump into Scarecrow.

'No, this is where I leave you,' croaked Jimmy. 'Creatures are not allowed inside. Go along with you.'

'Oh, please don't go,' began Mumfie, but the gaoler disappeared through the doorway and the door was slowly closing.

'Oh well,' sighed Mumfie. 'I suppose we'd better wait here and see what happens. I wish I didn't feel as though there were people watching us. After all, that door can't have opened quite by itself.'

'Oh don't. You make me quite nervous.' Poor Alfie was looking very nervous indeed. He was staring towards a long window overlooking the garden.

'Goodness!' he gasped. 'I'm sure I saw a face at that window a minute ago.'

'Where? Which window? I can't see anything.'

Mumfie was just going to investigate when there was a slight scratching noise against the pane, and he saw Scarecrow's face pressed against the glass. He trotted happily over to it. 'Here, help me open this, Alfie,' he ordered, looking round to make sure they were not watched. Between them they managed to pull the window open a little way. Scarecrow scrambled over the sill.

Mumfie hugged him. 'Oh, Scarecrow, it is lovely to see you. How clever of you to find me. This is Alfie;

I'm afraid he's got into trouble on my account. But, Scarecrow, were you quite wise to come inside?'

'I had to risk it,' said Scarecrow. 'It was probably my only chance of getting in.' He said 'Hullo' to Alfie, who was regarding him with great admiration.

'Mumfie,' he whispered, 'I've got an idea. A most tremendous idea. I heard the toad telling you that this was Night's garden. Well, then, this will be her palace.' He bent his head down to whisper in Mumfie's ear. 'If that's the case isn't it the most likely place for her Secretary to have hidden the professor's Magic. Either here or in the garden? If only we could find it then we could rescue all these poor people who have to be dreams.'

'Oo, my! Scarecrow. That *is* a good idea.' Mumfie jumped up and down. 'Quick, here's somebody coming.'

Scarecrow had only just time to slip behind a pillar when someone came down the hall.

Mumfie was quite surprised to see that it was only a small girl with a pale face and dark hair.

'Who are you waiting for?' she asked. 'Did anybody send for you?'

'I don't know who sent for us. The toad brought us along here and told us to wait until somebody came for us.'

'Oh, are you the prisoners?' The child looked at them with surprise. 'But we were told that one of them was most ferocious – a dangerous character. Which one of you is supposed to be dangerous? Neither of you look it.'

'I am,' said Mumfie rather proudly.

A muffled snigger came from behind the pillar where Scarecrow was hiding.

'What was that?' The child looked round. 'I'm sure I heard something.'

'Oh, that was only Alfie,' said Mumfie quickly. 'He's got giggles. He gets them from time to time. He can't help it.'

'Well, you'd better come along with me. I believe the Secretary is expecting you.'

'Do you live here?' Mumfie asked as the child led them through a cool courtyard in which a fountain was playing.

'Yes, I'm one of the attendants.'

'Are there any fish in that pool?'

'Yes, but do come along, if you hang over so far you'll fall in.'

She drew back some dark curtains and led the way into a room entirely surrounded by mirrors of blue glass. The floor was very cold and looked as though it were made of ice. Mumfie peeped at himself in one of the mirrors, and saw behind him a reflection of Scarecrow looking through the curtain. He hoped to goodness that the child would not look round. But she went over to a bench and began to put on a little pair of skates. She took two more pairs from a cupboard and pushed them over to Mumfie and Alfie. She noticed that Mumfie was rather bumbly, so she helped him to fix them on; then she started easily across the floor. Mumfie got up in a very wobbly manner, and promptly sat down again.

'Oh dear,' he giggled, 'this is rather difficult.'

He clung on to the bench and managed to get to his feet again.

'Do hurry up,' called the child. 'Oh, of course, I forgot you probably don't know how to skate.'

'No, I don't,' said Mumfie, breathing rather hard as he took a careful step forward. He was managing rather well on one leg if only the other one would have gone in the same direction. His feet, quite against his will got farther and farther apart, and he sat down again with a bump.

'Ow!' said Mumfie. 'I'm bumped. That's sore, that is. Why do all the floors have to be made of ice in this palace?'

'Well, what sort of floors do you have in your palaces?' asked the child. 'Or don't they have any palaces where you come from?'

'Of course they do,' said Mumfie indignantly. 'Hundreds and hundreds of them. But *we* manage to get quite a good polish up on wood.'

85

'Well, I suppose I'd better help you.' She caught hold of each of them by the arm and helped them across the floor.

Mumfie was wondering how ever Scarecrow would manage. He hoped that at least he would be able to find himself a pair of skates.

After a somewhat perilous journey they had crossed the wide floor. It was really a very lovely place to look at but terribly difficult to walk about in. Mumfie felt that skating should be rather fun if only he could get a little practice, but it was going to be very difficult to get about looking for the professor's magic; he knew that as soon as the child let him go he would fall down again, and Alfie was little better.

At last they reached some wide stairs, and

to his great relief the child told him to take his skates off.

'I think all that ice is very stupid in a palace,' he grumbled as he stuck out his foot to have the screws undone.

'It isn't stupid at all,' said the child. 'You can see for yourself how difficult it is for unauthorized persons to get in. What's more, it's a special sort of ice, so slippery that you can't possibly walk on it. Now just supposing there were someone following and trying to get in behind you: well, they wouldn't get very far, would they, because even if they could skate they wouldn't be likely to have any skates with them, and they wouldn't know where they were kept.'

Mumfie looked at her to see if she were only guessing, or if she had really seen Scarecrow behind them, but she had her back to him, and was unconcernedly undoing Alfie's skates.

Mumfie quickly fumbled in his pocket for the piece of paper with which he had thoughtfully provided himself. He wrote:

The skates are in a cubord just inside the big hall.

Then he screwed the paper up into a ball, trying not to make much crackle, and threw it across the hall. He watched it scudding across the ice, and then looked quickly the other way in the most unconcerned manner possible.

The child led them up some steep wide stairs, up and up, until Mumfie's legs began to ache. As he climbed he tore up little pieces of toffee paper and dropped them, to mark their way for Scarecrow.

'I didn't realize this palace was so tall,' he puffed. 'Is we ever going to get to the top?'

'Oh, YOU'LL never reach the top,' the child said. 'Nobody ever gets right up there except Night herself. Nobody else even knows quite how high it really is. I'll have to leave you here. You'll see the Secretary.'

She knocked at a door on one side of the endless

stairway. A dry far-away voice answered, 'Come in.'

'Well, good-bye,' she said. 'I don't expect I shall see you again.'

'Oh dear,' said Mumfie. 'Won't you be here when we come down?'

'Oh yes, I'll be here. If you DO come down.'

Mumfie did not like the sound of that at all. But she had opened the door.

'The prisoners, sir,' she said, and pushed them inside.

CHAPTER TEN

THE Secretary's room was gloomy and forbidding; it had a musty smell quite unlike the rest of the palace, which was fresh and airy. The only light came from a lamp with a clear blue flame which burned upon a desk at the far side of the room. Behind the desk was a long window covered by a curtain of some filmy material. Seated, bending over some papers, was the Secretary. He did not look up as they came in, but went on scratching with a quill pen. They waited for some time for him to speak, but he showed no sign that he was aware of their presence.

89

Mumfie thought that he had better speak first, but somehow the Secretary looked so forbidding that he dared not. After what seemed an age, he looked up. His face was quite colourless except for dark eyes that burned against its pallor, his long thin waxen hands stretched over the desk like claws, reminding Mumfie in some horrid way of a bat.

He reached across the desk for a pile of books, shuffling through them until he came to the one he was looking for. 'I will read the indictment,' he said in a harsh chilling voice.

'You, Mumfie, referred to as Public Enemy No. 1, are accused of the dreadful crime of spying.

'You, Alfie, referred to as Prisoner No. 2, are accused of aiding and abetting the aforesaid crime. What have you to say in your defence?'

'Plenty!' said Mumfie indignantly. 'I'm *not* spying and Alfie isn't aiding and whatever you saiding me.'

'Then if that is the case, you have no doubt some reasonable explanation for your presence here.'

'Yes, I have,' said Mumfie. 'I was talking to Alfie outside and we came in out of the draught, and just as I was leaving, a horrid old goblin came and caught hold of me and pulled me in again. Yes, *and* he tore my best coat at the same time. You can see for yourself.' He held up the front of his coat for the Secretary to see.

But the Secretary hardly glanced at the coat. He stared at Mumfie in such a terrifying manner that in spite of himself his knees began to tremble. Poor Alfie was shaking with fright, but he managed to blurt out:

'That's true, sir. Really it is. I know I shouldn't have asked him in, but it was terribly blowy outside and we were only just inside the tree-trunk; we weren't going any farther only Waxy came up and caught us.'

The Secretary turned in his chair to glare down at the unfortunate goblin.

'And what were you doing outside the tree?' he snapped. Poor Alfie was so frightened that his fat red face screwed up and he burst into tears.

'What were you doing?' repeated the Secretary in an awful voice. 'Answer me.'

But Mumfie had become so angry at the way his little friend was being bullied that he forgot to be frightened himself.

'He was taking a breath of fresh air.' He looked round the room. 'I don't suppose you know what that is, so you wouldn't understand,' he said rudely.

The Secretary rose from his chair. He looked more than ever like some monstrous bat as he swooped round the desk to tower over them. With a long skinny hand he reached out and picked Mumfie off his feet by the back of his collar.

'You will suffer for that,' he hissed. 'For those words you shall be condemned without trial.'

He dropped the frightened Mumfie down upon the floor and went over to the wall, where he pulled a long cord. From far away a bell clanged, and they heard heavy footsteps coming up the stairs. There was a knock at the door, and at the Secretary's impatient 'Come in,' a tall guard entered. Mumfie did not think that he had ever seen such an enormous man. He had a shaven head, a broken nose, and his ears curled about in a way that reminded Mumfie very much of cauli-flowers.

'Take them away,' snarled the Secretary. 'Lock them in the Tower from which there is No Return.'

'Wot, them?' said the guard, evidently surprised.

'Do as you're told,' ordered the Secretary coldly.

'Got to 'ave an order,' said the guard. 'Can't put 'em in there without an order.'

The Secretary sat down at his desk and they watched his scratching quill fly over the paper.

'Here is your order, and see that it is obeyed.'

The guard took the paper, and looked at it rather reluctantly.

'Seems in order, though what you want to put them little 'uns in there for beats me,' he mumbled under his breath. He picked up the trembling Mumfie under one arm, and the sobbing Alfie under the other, and marched out of the room with them without so much as another glance at the Secretary. He kicked the door to behind him with his large hobnailed boot.

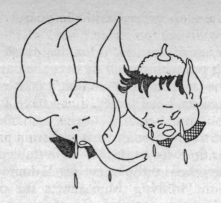

'Well, I suppose I'll have to take you up there,' he said.

'Oh, must you?' asked Mumfie hopefully. 'Couldn't you manage somehow to lose us half-way up?'

'Don't see how I can, not with this 'ere written order. If it weren't for that I'm about sick of taking orders from that mean old buzzard what I could knock unconscious with the flat of me 'and. But he'll see that a copy goes in to the Lady herself and then if I 'av'n't delivered you intact to the proper place, I'll be for it.'

All this time he had been laboriously mounting stairs; hundreds of them – it seemed as if they would never stop.

'Aren't we ever coming to the top?' asked Mumfie presently. It was rather uncomfortable being carried; he wished that the guard would put him down.

'I wonder why they don't have a lift?' he said.

At last the guard stopped before a very small door. If only he would put them down when he unlocked it then perhaps they could make a dash down the stairs. But he did not let them go, instead he tucked them both firmly under one arm while he unlocked the door with a key which he took from a hook on the wall.

'Oh dear,' said Mumfie, 'I don't want to go in there. Please don't put us in.'

'Can't be helped, I'm afraid,' said the guard. 'Orders is orders, but I'll see if I can have a word with the Lady on your behalf. It seems a shame that you should be stuck in there and left without a proper trial. In the meantime, in you go.'

He pushed them through the small door and shut it behind them. They heard him muttering to himself as he turned the key in the lock.

Poor Alfie was snuffling miserably, and a tear fell unbidden from Mumfie's eye and plopped on to his coat. He brushed it aside angrily, this would never do. But it felt terribly lonely up there in the tower all by themselves; it was utterly quiet except for the wind licking against the tall window. Mumfie went over to it and looked out. To his great surprise he could see thousands of stars piercing the dark sky like sequins.

'My goodness, Alfie, but we must be up above the ground; in fact, it looks as though we're right up in the air. I wish it wasn't so dark in here. They can't just be going to leave us here for ever and ever.'

'What about your friend?' said Alfie hopefully. 'P'r'aps he was able to follow us as far as the Secretary's room and overhear what happened to us.'

'I'm afraid that depends a good deal on whether he found the skates,' said Mumfie. He told Alfie about the note he had written. He tried to talk as much as he could in order to keep up their courage. He even suggested that they sing a few songs, as that was a good way to keep cheerful. They began the Tree in a Wood song because that went on longer than any that they knew; but it was no good, they just had not the heart to go on singing. They sat down in the darkness and waited miserably, hoping against hope that Scarecrow would find them.

CHAPTER ELEVEN

SCARECROW, peeping through the curtains, saw
Mumfie's note sliding across the floor. He waited until
they were out of sight, and then managed to sweep it
towards him with the broom. It did not take him long
to find the cupboard where the skates were kept; he
chose a pair that fitted him reasonably well, and put
them on. 'Now for it,' he said to himself. He had done
some roller-skating once and hoped that this would be
rather the same thing. To his delight he managed quite
well. He rushed across the floor at a great rate; the only
difficulty was how to stop himself when he came to the

other side of the room. He settled that question quite unexpectedly by sitting down with a bump. He took off his skates and hid them under a bench, then started to climb up the stairs. The little pieces of toffee paper that Mumfie had dropped marked their way quite clearly. 'Oh, these stairs,' muttered Scarecrow to himself. His legs after a while had begun to ache and he would very much have liked to sit down for a rest. At last the toffee paper stopped outside a door. Scarecrow bent his head down to listen. He heard the grating voice of the Secretary, and Mumfie's rather squeaky replies, but he could not make out what they were saying.

Presently a bell clanged out and went echoing away down the stairs. He thought he heard a door open somewhere below, and footsteps creaking up towards him.

'Crackers!' said Scarecrow in a fright. He looked round for somewhere to hide and had just time to scramble on to the long window-sill and get behind the curtain when the guard appeared and went into the room.

Scarecrow waited until presently he emerged with Mumfie and Alfie, one under each arm; then he crept up the stairs after them. He had never climbed so many stairs in his life; he quite envied Mumfie being carried. He waited until the guard had pushed his prisoners in through the small door, then, as soon as they were inside dashed up the stairs and round a bend so that he should be out of the way when the guard came out. He watched him hang up the key on its hook by the door, and then waited patiently until he was out of sight. He then went over for the key, unlocked the door and went inside.

It was so dark that at first he could not see, but presently he made out Mumfie and Alfie sitting side by side on the floor looking very dejected.

'Mumfie,' he whispered, 'it's ME.'

Mumfie bounced up with a squeal of delight. He rushed over to Scarecrow and flung his arms around him. Then his face fell.

'Oh dear, oh dear, have they captured you too? I was afraid they would see you coming up behind us.'

'No fear.' Scarecrow swung the key. 'The guard left this outside and I've come to let you out. Mumfie, I can't help feeling we ought to go on up these stairs until we come to the top. It's an awful thought, my legs are so stiff that I very much doubt if my knees will go on bending much longer, but I'm sure it's the most likely place for the Secretary to have hidden anything that he doesn't want found.'

'I spec's that is where Night lives,' put in Alfie. 'I've often heard some of the old goblins talking about a mysterious tower, but they always used to shut up if any of us younger ones were about. But don't you think we had better get out of here whilst we still have the chance; if we go on up the stairs we may get caught again, and that would be awful.'

Mumfie looked at Scarecrow and Scarecrow looked at Mumfie.

'Look, Alfie,' Scarecrow began, 'I do agree with what you say, and it's a shame to drag you into this; after all, it's really on our account that you've got into all this trouble so far. You go back, there's a good fellow. Mumfie and I will be all right, we'll just have a look to see what is up there and then we will follow you down.'

'No,' said Alfie, interrupting, 'no, I won't. I'm not going to leave you in the lurch now. Besides, I don't like going down there all by myself, I'd rather we all stayed together.'

But Mumfie was pacing up and down the cell thinking hard.

'Listen, Scarecrow, I tell you what would be a good idea, if only Alfie could get back and manage to see the professor and tell him what's happening, then the old gentleman could be getting all ready with his spell pots and things, so that he can make the magic just as soon as we get it to him. Could you do that, Alfie?'

Alfie looked rather doubtful, but it would never do to show any sign of fear in front of the brave and clever Scarecrow.

'Yes, I think so,' he said. 'Only what shall I do if you don't find the magic, and you get caught again?'

'You could tell the professor all about everything that has happened 'til now. He is so clever that he might be able to think of some way to help us.' It was a comforting thought that the professor would at least know where they were.

'Well,' said Alfie, 'if I'm going I'd better

go. I do hope you'll be all right and that we'll meet again later on.'

'Oh, we'll be all right,' said Scarecrow cheerfully. 'We've got out of just as bad places as this before now. Good-bye for now, and good luck.' He patted Alfie on the back by way of encouragement, and they watched him patter quietly down the stairs. They waited until he was out of sight round a bend, then they began the long ascent.

'Oo, Scarecrow, I'm glad we're together again,' said Mumfie happily, during one of their pauses for breath. 'This is rather fun. I do hope we'll find the magic. Have you any idea what magic looks like, Scarecrow?'

'Yes,' replied Scarecrow airily, though as a matter of fact he had but the haziest notion.

'In the first place, it's usually in a box. A magic box is quite different from other boxes,' he added by way of explanation.

'How different?'

'Well, it just doesn't look like ordinary boxes, and you can't open it like ordinary boxes, because it's locked by magic instead of with a key.' He was rather proud of that; he felt it to be a very good description of a magic box indeed.

Mumfie looked at him admiringly. 'I'm glad you know what it looks like,' he said. 'That will be very helpful while we are trying to find it. Oo, look at this big window.'

They seemed at last to have reached the top of the stairs; they had come out upon a wide landing, walled on one side by a window.

'It's much lighter,' said Scarecrow. 'Mumfie, I do believe we're right up in the sky and dawn is beginning to break.'

Into the sky's greyness filtered a long streak of light; Mumfie peeped out of the window trying to see what was below. As he watched, a window far below them opened and a dark shape fluttered out from it.

'Oh, look, Scarecrow, what is it? It's flying up here, higher and higher. Oh mercy, it's a great bat, the biggest one I've ever seen. Oh my goodness, I'm glad the window's shut.'

The great bat was coming nearer and nearer, zig-zagging through the air. Scarecrow pulled Mumfie to one side.

'Better get out of sight,' he whispered. 'You never know. It's such a very big bat. It wouldn't do for any-one to find us up here.'

The great webbed wings of the bat threw their dark shadow across the window panes. Mumfie, crouching

down, gave a gasp of fright. The creature's head was turned towards them and the face was strangely like the face of the Secretary.

'Oh, go away, go away,' muttered Mumfie in a fright. He hid his face in Scarecrow's coat.

'Has it gone?' he asked presently.

'Yes, it's gone all right. Hanging about outside like that, the old Nosey Parker,' Scarecrow sniffed. He noticed that Mumfie was still looking rather frightened.

'Don't be scared, old chap,' he said comfortingly; 'it can't get inside. Come on, let's have a look for this magic. It's lucky there doesn't seem to be anyone about.'

He crossed the landing towards a wonderful door carved entirely from pink jade.

'Well, it's rather a problem to know how to open it.' He regarded the door intently. 'There doesn't seem to be a handle of any kind.'

'Perhaps this carving like the branch of a tree is the handle,' suggested Mumfie, taking hold of it. 'It sticks out rather.' The jade felt cold to his hand, but as he touched it, to his delight the door began to swing open. They slipped through it and went inside.

They found themselves in a beautiful shaded room from the centre of which sprang a gleaming milky stairway carved in a spiral that twisted up out of sight. As they watched, a lovely girl came down the steps. Her hair was pale as spun glass, and from her there came soft rays of light. She stopped as she caught sight of them and half turned as though to go up the stairs again.

There was no good in their trying to hide since she had seen them; besides, she looked just as frightened as they at the sudden meeting.

Scarecrow was gazing at her with astonishment; she was so beautiful that he could not think of anything to say, but just stood gaping.

'Good morning,' said Mumfie politely. 'I do hope we didn't disturb you.'

The girl came down the steps and walked towards them, shedding her strange light around her.

'Who are you?' she asked. 'You look too real for Dreams.'

Mumfie was just going to say that they were not dreams, when Scarecrow poked him. As well to be careful, as they did not know if the lovely girl was friendly disposed towards them.

'We were just looking for something,' he said hastily. 'Please don't let us disturb you.'

'You have got a lovely frock on,' Mumfie could not help saying, as he stared at the soft gleaming white draperies with admiration.

She smiled at him. 'It is nice,' she said. 'All the Moonbeams wear them. Do tell me what it is that you are looking for, perhaps I could help you to find it.'

Mumfie looked at Scarecrow inquiringly. After frowning a moment Scarecrow nodded.

'Well, as a matter of fact, we're looking for something of the professor's,' said Mumfie, speaking very fast. 'Only don't tell Night, because we are supposed to be locked up and I don't know what would happen to us if . . .'

But the moonbeam girl broke into what he was saying. She caught hold of him by the arm.

'Which professor?' she asked earnestly, shaking him. 'Which professor do you mean? Oh, tell me quickly.'

'The nice one that lives in the forest,' said Mumfie.

'But how did you meet him? How did you come

here? Oh, do please tell me, I'll do anything to help you.'

'Do you know him?' asked Mumfie hopefully. This was indeed lucky; it looked as though she were quite prepared, even eager, to be friendly.

She looked round about her nervously. 'I wasn't always a moonbeam,' she whispered. 'Please tell me quickly how you came here.'

Mumfie and Scarecrow began to tell her the story as quickly as they could. When they had finished her lovely face was shining with excitement.

'You see,' she explained, 'before Night chose me for one of her Moonbeams I used to be the professor's granddaughter. Of course, it was a very great honour to be chosen, and I thought at the time how lovely and exciting it would be, but now I know that I'd much rather be an ordinary person playing at home in Grandpapa's garden. But do you really think the Secretary could have hidden his magic up here? I think myself that it's quite likely, because you see up these stairs is Night's private apartment. Nobody is ever allowed inside it. I have sometimes seen a brilliant light coming from under the door, and they do say that the Moon comes to visit her there, but nobody else but the Secretary would ever dare go in. It's dreadful how he bullies her, he's getting more and more powerful; in fact, they say that he wants to be the Lord of Darkness himself. But you mustn't go up there, something dreadful might happen. P'r'aps he's hidden it in some other room,' she suggested hopefully.

'I shouldn't think that's very likely,' said Scarecrow, nervously regarding the stairs.

Mumfie agreed with him. It was far more likely that

he would hide an important secret in the very place where one would be least likely to find it. He looked at the stairs with a very determined expression, and began slowly to mount them.

'Oh dear, it's no use your trying to get in,' said the girl, catching hold of him. 'You see, when Night is away she always leaves her dog on guard, and if you so much as attempted to approach the door it would tear you in pieces.'

'Oo-ER!' said Mumfie. 'That makes it a bit awkward, doesn't it, Scarecrow? But I usually gets on very well with dogs,' he added thoughtfully.

'Well, I *don't*,' said Scarecrow with finality. 'Dogs have an entirely unnecessary habit of thinking I'm a tramp. I can't think why, but they do.'

'Well, I'm just going up to have a look at this dog,' said Mumfie bravely, though he was feeling very far from brave inside. He started up the stairs again. Scarecrow gave a heavy sigh and followed slowly behind him.

CHAPTER TWELVE

MUMFIE went up the stairs as quietly as he could with his legs wobbling. He wished his knees would not shake so. He looked round to see if Scarecrow were following, and was grateful to see him close behind.

'What do dogs specially like, Scarecrow?' he whispered.

'Bones,' answered Scarecrow lugubriously; 'I only hope he doesn't get any of mine.'

'Do dogs like stuffing, Scarecrow?'

'Probably,' said Scarecrow in a dismal voice. 'Here, we're near the top. Can you see any sign of the brute?'

'No, but I can hear him.'

It was evident that the dog had sensed their presence already, though they were still round a bend in the stairway, for he began to growl in a low rumbling manner which they did not care for at all. Scarecrow turned round and went down a few steps.

'Come on, Mumfie,' he said. 'I don't know about you, but I've no intention of ending *my* life as a dog's supper.'

'But, Scarecrow, we *can't* go back now, not when we've got so far. He may sound fiercer than he is.' Mumfie caught hold of Scarecrow to pull him up the stairs.

'Oh, all right,' said Scarecrow with resignation. 'But it's quite against my better judgment.'

They rounded the last bend, scarcely daring to breathe, and saw stretched across a doorway an immense white bulldog, which upon seeing them got to its feet and emitted a truly terrible growl. It stood motionless, waiting for them to move.

Scarecrow again made to descend the stairs; he had had quite enough of this. There was obviously no

chance of getting by the brute, and little sense that he could see in going on just to get torn to pieces. But to his horror he saw Mumfie walk a few steps forward, making the sort of noises that one makes to dogs. 'Hello. Nice dog,' he said in the most friendly voice he could manage.

The dog went on growling, but still did not move.

Scarecrow dared not speak for fear of angering it further. He watched Mumfie, fascinated. Mumfie went on, still making doggy noises and holding out his hand. He was quite close to the animal when, to Scarecrow's horror, it gave a great bound, leaping at Mumfie with such force that it knocked him flat over backwards.

'Oh, for mercy's sake,' gasped Scarecrow, rushing to the rescue. 'I knew this would happen.'

Mumfie had just time to scramble to his feet when the animal rushed again. Then he noticed a very peculiar fact. The bulldog's stumpy tail was wagging furiously. It put out a large red tongue and licked his face.

'Oh, Scarecrow,' sang Mumfie in delight, 'I believe he only wants to play.' He laughed aloud with excitement and happiness. 'He's only rough because he's so big. Aren't you? Nice dog.'

The bulldog was rushing around in circles. It turned its attention to Scarecrow and had no difficulty at all in knocking him over.

'Here!' said Scarecrow, picking himself up. 'Don't be so violent.' The bulldog waddled back to Mumfie, pushing itself against him and wagging its tail. Mumfie looked from the dog to the door. 'Do you think he'd try to stop us if we went inside?' he asked.

'I don't expect so if we go in in a matter-of-fact manner. Let's try it.' He opened the door, but the dog

was too busy bouncing round Mumfie to pay any attention.

'I think it's a nice dog,' said Mumfie happily, patting it with one hand and firmly holding on to its collar with the other until Scarecrow was safely inside. Then he followed, the dog behind him still wagging its tail. Mumfie pushed the door to behind him, leaving it open just a little way so that they could get out easily. They looked carefully round to see that no one was inside.

It was the strangest room. Round the walls were big glass cases lined with some dark blue material against which hung, sparkling, hundreds of stars of all different shapes and sizes. On a table were bowls of jade and amber, filled with a strange fine sparkling dust. It was dreadfully cold, Mumfie shivered and pulled his coat closer about him. Scarecrow's teeth were chattering so that he was afraid someone would hear them.

'Come on,' he whispered, 'we'd better start looking. You begin at that side of the room and I'll take the other.'

He went over to a long chest and lifted the lid. He rummaged about in it, but it seemed to be filled with strange-looking things that looked just like huge candle extinguishers. Mumfie on his side was having very little luck. He looked in all the star cases and in several cupboards, in chairs and under cushions; he had very nearly met Scarecrow again, and was getting quite despairing when he found several large ledgers piled up against the wall. He peeped inside the top one and it was just like a story book filled with rather strange pictures like the ones he had seen in the room below. He wanted to go on looking through the books, but it was evident that no magic box could be hidden in them.

'I don't believe it's anywhere up here,' he said sadly.
'There doesn't seem anywhere else to look.'

'Did you look in all those star cabinets?' asked
Scarecrow. Mumfie nodded. 'Oo, look. I wonder what
this is.' He went over to a big round crystal globe that
was standing on a beautifully carved pillar in a dark
corner of the room.

At that moment the dog, who had lain down by the
door, suddenly sprang up with an angry snarl. Mumfie
got such a fright that he jumped sideways. He felt
something rocking away from him and put out his
hand blindly to save it, but there was a terrific crash
and the crystal dashed to the ground, where it burst
into a thousand fragments. As it touched the hard floor
the room was for an instant flooded with a brilliant
light, then they were plunged in thick frightening
darkness. Mumfie stood rooted to the spot, hardly
daring to breathe. A faint square of light appeared

through the slowly opening door. He did not know what he should do, for in that instant of blazing light he had seen amongst the shattered fragments of the crystal a small dark box. There was no time to pick it up, though he could feel it against his foot. He did the next best thing, he flopped to the ground and sat down upon it, pushing it under his coat. He was only just in time. The door stood wide, revealing outlined against the light the sombre bat-like form of the Secretary.

He came into the room, peering before him in the darkness. Slowly towards Mumfie he advanced, the whites of his eyes gleaming in the darkness. Mumfie sat perfectly still, thinking that his last hour had come. The Secretary suddenly emitted a low snarl and sprang forward. At that moment Scarecrow, who had flattened himself against the wall, leapt forward and flung himself with all his force upon the villain's back, so that, taken entirely by surprise, he stumbled forward and measured his length upon the ground.

Mumfie leapt up, calling to the dog to help him, whilst Scarecrow and the Secretary struggled together in a tangled heap.

Suddenly he saw his opportunity. The Secretary with his far superior strength had managed to get the gallant Scarecrow underneath him, and was doing his best to choke him. Mumfie rushed up, and raising the

black box high, brought it down with all his strength upon the enemy's unprotected head. He gave a groan and fell back upon the ground with arms outstretched.

'Well, that's *him* settled,' said Mumfie with satisfaction. 'Come on, Scarecrow. We'd better get out of this, quick.'

'Thanks, old fellow,' said Scarecrow hoarsely, feeling at his throat and straightening his much disordered neck-tie.

'But we still haven't got that magic, and I don't know how we are going to find it in this gloom. By the way, whatever did you find to bang him with?'

'I don't know what it is,' said Mumfie excitedly, 'but it's a most successful banger. It's a box, Scarecrow. Are you sure you'd know what a magic box would look like, if you saw one?'

'Yes,' said Scarecrow airily. ' 'Least I think I would. Come on, we'd better hurry up; bring the box with you, Mumfie, just in case.'

They ran out of the room, shutting the door behind them. Down the stairs and through the crystal room, they looked round for the Moonbeam girl, but she had disappeared; they dared not stop to look for her. When they reached the outer landing dawn had broken over the sky; the first soft blue was appearing. They stopped at the window and looked out, for the strangest procession was floating towards them through the pale sky, an endless stream of People, Animals, and Things, drifting down nearer and nearer until the leaders came so close to the window that their floating garments brushed against the glass.

'It's the Dreams coming back,' whispered Scarecrow. 'If only we could make sure this is the magic, and stop them somehow before the goblins take charge of them again. Quick – look in the box, Mumfie.'

Mumfie tried to open the box, but to his dismay it was locked.

'But it can't be locked,' he said, puzzled. 'Because look, Scarecrow, there isn't a key-hole.'

'Then you can be sure it's the magic box' – Scarecrow looked wise – 'because as I told you, magic boxes never have any keys; they're always locked by magic.'

'Oh, then the professor will surely know how to open it.' Mumfie put it safely under his coat and they hurried down the endless stairs, flight after flight. It seemed that they would never get to the bottom.

'Wish there was banisters,' puffed Mumfie as he trotted after Scarecrow, who was leaping down two steps at a time. He envied his friend's long legs, and tried to manage two at a time himself, but they were just too deep for him; he got caught up in his own feet and down he went bumpity bump, head over heels. He called to Scarecrow to look out, but too late. He banged right into him in his flight, so that Scarecrow was

bowled over and went rolling down too. Faster and
faster they flew, until at
last they landed at the
bottom with a bump.

'Well, at least that was
a quicker way of doing
it,' gasped Scarecrow.
'Are you hurt, Mumfie?'

'No, not hurt,' said
Mumfie, carefully picking
himself up and making
sure that the precious box
was safe. 'Only bumped.
Oh dear, now we've got
to cross this slippery floor,
and I'm not very good at
it, Scarecrow, even if I
can find where she put
my skates.'

'I hid mine under the
bench when I came
in.'

Scarecrow began to fix
them on. 'Come on,
Mumfie, climb on the seat
and I'll give you a pick-
a-back. I think I can
manage.'

Mumfie climbed on to Scarecrow's back whilst he
stood up and wobbled about a bit, trying to get his
balance, but at last he managed to push off, and shot
across the floor at a terrific rate. They were only just in
time; they heard someone clattering down the stairs
behind them. Mumfie peeped back fearfully and saw

one of the guards at the edge of the ice floor. He was waving frantically, calling out to them to stop.

'Don't wobble!' said Scarecrow through his teeth; 'if I over-balance now we're done.' He gave an awful slither and bent nearly over backwards, but just managed to right himself. He reached the edge, where he dropped Mumfie down and kicked off the skates. They rushed through the hall to the entrance door, which by some extraordinary good fortune was open. Mumfie slammed the door behind them and they dashed away into the garden, dodging amongst the trees.

'Can you remember the way you came?' called Scarecrow. 'I couldn't find the way out.'

Mumfie nodded. 'I think so. Oh dear, I can hear people running. They're after us, Scarecrow.'

They hurried their steps until they were soon lost to sight from their pursuers amongst the tall blue trees.

CHAPTER THIRTEEN

'OH my goodness!' gasped Mumfie, 'I think I've lost the door, it ought to be just by here. Whatever are we to do?'

'Wait a minute,' whispered Scarecrow. 'I thought I saw something flash through the trees over there. We'd better be careful.' He pulled Mumfie behind a tree as they heard feet pattering towards them. A voice was calling softly something that sounded very like 'Mumfie.'

'Did you hear that, Scarecrow? I'm sure they said Mumfie. Listen.'

Again, louder this time, came the call. 'Mumfie.' This time there was no mistaking it. Mumfie was emerging from behind the tree when Scarecrow pulled him back. 'Take care, it may be a trap,' he whispered.

'It's not a trap. It's Alfie,' said Mumfie delightedly, running out to meet the small figure that was waddling towards them.

'Oh, I'm so glad I've found you,' cried Alfie, hugging him. He looked very much as though he would like to hug Scarecrow too, but thought better of it. It seemed rather disrespectful.

'Did you get it?' he asked as he led the way towards the garden door.

'Yes,' whispered Mumfie, 'it's safe in my pocket, but I'm afraid they are after us. What had we better do now?'

For answer Alfie ran over to the door of the puzzle hall and pushed it open.

'But we mustn't go in there,' said Mumfie nervously. 'The clerk may be at his desk, and then he would give the alarm.'

'He is at his desk,' said Alfie with emphasis, 'but he won't give no alarm.'

They followed him into the room, and there sitting at his desk with all his ink-bottles before him was the clerk. His arms were bound to the sides of his chair, and his mouth was securely gagged.

'Oh, poor thing,' cried Mumfie. 'He does look uncomfy.'

'It's all right,' said Alfie happily, 'it's only toffee. He agreed to being gagged, in fact it was his own suggestion, because otherwise he would have felt bound to give the alarm, and he is really quite friendly towards us. He'll eat through the toffee presently, and then he'll feel more comfortable. Won't you?' he turned to the clerk, who nodded his head and went on placidly chewing his gag.

'But what are we doing here?' asked Scarecrow.

'Oughtn't we to be hurrying to the professor whilst the going's good?'

'The professor and me thought of a better plan,' said Alfie proudly. 'I managed to get through to him and tell him that you were looking for his magic, and he suggested that I should come back and assemble all the small goblins and the Dreams, who you see are themselves in the daytime. The professor cannot use his magic until night falls and they are Dreams again. He guessed that you might have got into serious trouble before then, and so I've collected all these people to help you.'

'Well, I must congratulate you,' said Scarecrow, his eyes gleaming with excitement at the thought of a possible battle. Alfie swelled with pride. 'Thank you very much,' he said. 'It wasn't all my own idea,' he added honestly, 'some of it was the professor's.'

He led the way into the puzzle hall, and there

assembled were all the Dreams regarding the entrance expectantly. When Mumfie and Scarecrow appeared in the doorway there was a prolonged burst of cheering. A great many small goblins disengaged themselves from the group and rushed forward.

'Have they got it?' they chorused anxiously.

For answer Mumfie took the black box from under his coat and waved it above his head. There was a perfect roar of cheers from the Dreams and goblins. 'Whoopee!' bellowed a very small goblin, jumping up and down.

Scarecrow shouted to try and make himself heard above the din. He climbed up on to one of the tables and waved his arms for silence.

'Hadn't we better hold a council of war?' he suggested. 'The enemy are already hot on our tracks, and we must have some plan of action, otherwise we shall just get in a muddle and it will be easy to defeat us.'

'Hear! hear!' said Mumfie firmly. 'Hadn't we better lock the door until we're ready, Scarecrow?'

'Yes, lock the door,' cried several of the goblins. 'We'd better barricade it also. Oh my, we don't know how to lock it, we haven't got the key.'

'That door doesn't lock with a key,' said Mumfie. 'It blows shut and sucks open. If we were to stuff something into the key-hole so that it couldn't be blown through, then they can't open it.'

This was hailed as a good idea, and they began looking round for something to stuff it with.

'What about me?' said a long thin sausage, coming up. 'I'm very often used as stuffing.' His offer was greeted with applause and two goblins picked him up and pushed him carefully through the key-hole.

'Now,' said Scarecrow. 'If it comes to a battle, what

are we going to use for ammunition? You can bet all the old goblins and guards will be armed.'

Everybody looked at everybody else, and their faces fell. They had no arms of any sort, nothing even that they could throw. They all began to talk at once, but no one had any helpful suggestion to offer. Mumfie, who had climbed up on the table besides Scarecrow, marched up and down, thinking hard. Suddenly he had an idea.

'Wait a minute,' he called, but everyone was making such a noise with their chattering that he could not make himself heard.

'Silence!' bellowed Scarecrow. 'Mumfie has an idea. They are usually good,' he added, looking at Mumfie expectantly.

Mumfie stooped down and picked up one of the pieces of a puzzle that was still spread out on the table.

'What about these?' he suggested. 'There's hundreds and hundreds of them. Enough to equip a whole army.'

His idea was greeted with shouts of delight. Everyone rushed for the puzzles, tearing them apart and stuffing every available space and cranny about their persons with as many pieces as they could carry. There was a special demand for the nightmare puzzles as they were much heavier, and their pieces more jagged.

Scarecrow and Mumfie

were just completing their equipment when there was a loud hammering on the outer door. Mumfie removed the sausage, with a word of thanks, and ran out to the clerk's desk where he seized up a bottle of red ink and the clerk's fountain-pen filler. He stuffed these in his smallest pocket, and stood ready for the fight.

Scarecrow was busy marshalling everybody into a good fighting square, when there was a splintering of wood and the outer door burst open. In rushed a horde of the old goblins, led by an immense guard; but they had not time to more than raise their bows and arrows when they were greeted with a hail of flying puzzle pieces, which took them so by surprise that those in front fell down on top of one another, getting in the way of the rearguard so that they could not squeeze through the narrow door.

'Drive them back,' roared Scarecrow, flinging a bunch of nightmares at an infuriated goblin who had managed to scramble over the rest, and was encouraging the others to follow him. At that moment Mumfie caught sight of Waxy who was laying about him in a towering rage.

'I'll get you!' he muttered into his beard. 'I'll get you for this.' He made a bee-line for Alfie, who was very much enjoying himself throwing ammunition at everybody at once, and letting out loud war-whoops. He raised his truncheon and was just going to bring it down full on the unfortunate Alfie's head when Mumfie pulled out his fountain-pen filler and caught him neatly in the eye with a large dollop of red ink.

'OW!' said Waxy, dropping the truncheon to rub his finger in his eye. Alfie seized the weapon and gave the old goblin a good buffet with it so that he sat down upon the floor with a very surprised expression on his face and then appeared to be going to sleep.

The battle raged fast and furious, the Dreams, led by Mumfie and Scarecrow, were gradually forcing the enemy back into the circular hall and out into the passage.

'Drive them out into the woods,' commanded Scarecrow.

Bang! bang! went Mumfie, who had got hold of somebody's truncheon. Bang! Whack! Bang! 'This is fun,' he puffed, neatly avoiding a blow from an enormous guard.

At last they had them on the run, the goblins were getting tired of being whacked about and were pouring into the passage where they made straight for the door. The guards tried to rally them but could not hold them. They put up a last effort of resistance, but

Mumfie kept them at bay with spurts of red ink. He hoped they would soon turn as the bottle was getting very low, and the puzzle pieces were running out. Shouting and whooping, they drove them down the corridor and up the stairs higgledy-piggledy to the outer door which burst open as the frightened goblins beat against it, tumbling them out into the woods, where they fled to right and left, disappearing amongst the trees.

The small goblins wanted to go on chasing them, and Scarecrow had some ado to collect them in an orderly array.

'Now we must go for the professor,' he said. 'Look, it's beginning to get dark, we'll have to hurry up. You must stay here and guard the entrance in case they should rally again, though I rather doubt that; they looked as if they'd had about enough of that for one day.

'Mumfie and I will go to the professor's cottage and give him the magic, then we'll bring him back here. Come on, Mumfie. Alfie, I shall leave you in charge.

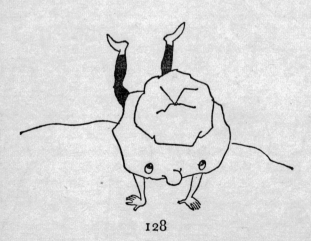

See that everyone keeps in good order and don't let anyone get out of hand.' He frowned rather severely at Bread, who was behaving in an idiotic manner, dancing about on his head, and letting out shrill squeaking cries. 'If he doesn't stop that soon you'd better throw some water over him to quieten him down a bit.'

They were turning to go, when Mrs. Pig, who had been extremely useful in the battle, flying about and landing suddenly on the enemy from above, pushed her way through the crowd towards them.

'I know you'll be very busy,' she said; 'but could you possibly find time to bring Pinkey along with the professor, I don't think he ought to be left in the cottage by himself with all those wild goblins in the woods?'

'Yes, of course we will,' said Mumfie. 'He can come in somebody's pocket, that is if he's asleep, which is more than likely. Come on, Scarecrow.'

He took hold of Scarecrow's hand and they pattered off through the woods towards the professor's cottage.

CHAPTER FOURTEEN

'IT'S really beginning to get quite dark,' said Scarecrow, looking up amongst the trees. 'We'd better watch out, Mumfie, we don't want one of those old goblins to jump out and bump us off at this stage of the proceedings.'

'Oh no, certainly not,' said Mumfie decidedly. 'That would never do, but look, I've still got my truncheon. I'm quite glad I brought it along.'

'And me mine.' Scarecrow brandished it. 'Goodness, it's getting quite hard to find the way. Are you sure we're on the right path, Mumfie?'

But just as he said it they came out into the clearing to see the professor's twisted cottage before them. Mumfie ran up to the door hugging the precious box to him under his coat.

'Oo, won't he be excited when we give him back his magic again?' he said happily. He opened the front door and ran into the cottage, Scarecrow close on his heels.

'Mr. Professor,' he sang out. 'It's me, Mumfie. Where are you?' There was no answer so he pushed open the door of the study and went in.

It was dark in the room, but the professor was sitting at his desk with his back towards them. He did not look round as they came in.

'Here we are,' said Mumfie, running over to him. 'And look, we've brought you your . . .' Then he stopped dead, for at that moment the professor turned round. To their horror it was not the professor at all, but the pale gleaming face of the Secretary.

'You've brought me my what?' said the Secretary.

'I haven't brought you anything,' said Mumfie indignantly. 'And what are you doing here? This isn't your house. Where's the professor?'

The Secretary suddenly sprang up. 'Give me that box,' he hissed. He stretched out his claw-like hand.

'What box?' said Scarecrow quickly. 'I don't know what you're talking about, but I'll give you something else if you don't hurry up and tell us where the professor is.' He waved his truncheon in a threatening manner.

'Well,' said the Secretary, sitting down again, 'it

131

appears that we must come to terms. You want the professor; I want that box which one of you is carrying. You hand over the box, and I will hand over the professor.'

`Scarecrow thought quickly; this was a very awkward turn of events. Whatever had the villain done to the poor professor? He must be hiding him somewhere, but how were they to find him?

'Come on,' said the Secretary, 'hand over that box. If you do not give it to me within the next ten seconds it will be the worse for your precious professor.'

'Why?' asked Mumfie, frightened. 'What are you going to do to him? You can't hurt him; he never did you any harm.'

'Oh, can't I,' said the Secretary, grinning. 'We'll see about that, and to prove my point I will tell you just where he is. At this very moment he is down the well in his own bucket – half-way down, that is. Do you see this cord?' He touched a length of rope that was tied to the table-leg just by his chair.

'The other end of this is secured to the bucket. If you look you will see it going over the window-sill. Now if I cut the cord it will release the bucket and down into the water will fall the silly old man. And it's a very deep well, so they tell me,' he added nastily.

'Now how about handing over that box. I shall

132

count up to ten, and when I reach ten I shall cut the cord.'

'And if we do give you the box,' gasped Scarecrow, 'then what will you do?'

'Then I shall remove myself from this rather dingy cottage with all haste, and leave you to rescue the old man from his bucket in any manner that you see fit.' He took a large clasp-knife from his pocket and slowly opened it. Then brandishing it in the air perilously near the cord, he began to count.

'ONE!

TWO!'

'Oh, whatever shall we do?' Scarecrow and Mumfie looked at each other in dismay. If they gave him the box he would fly away with it and then they would be back where they started, but they could not let the poor professor fall into the well, where he would surely be drowned. Oh, whatever were they to do?

'THREE!'

Poor Mumfie was jumping up and down in his agitation, his little fists clenched.

'FOUR!'

He burst into tears. 'Oh! Oh! Oh!' he sobbed. 'This is awful.' He stuffed his hand into his pocket to find his hankie, and felt something inside it. He took a deep breath.

'I'll give you the box,' he said.

Scarecrow looked at him with amazement, but he refused to return the look.

The Secretary stopped counting. 'Ah-ha!' he said, not troubling to conceal his triumph. 'Now you are talking. Well, hurry up and hand it over, I've no time to waste.'

'Oh dear,' said Mumfie, fumbling about, 'I've got

it tucked into my jumper and I don't seem to be able to get it out. Could you help me?'

'I'll help you,' said the Secretary. 'Come over here where I can reach you.' Mumfie came round to stand before him.

'It's there in my jumper,' he said. 'You get it out.'

The Secretary stooped down and began feeling about with his long skinny hands in the folds of Mumfie's coat. As he stooped, quick as lightning Mumfie fished in his pocket, and seizing the fountain-pen filler, squirted the rest of the ink full into the Secretary's face. The villain snatched his hands up towards his eyes; he floundered about, blinded by the ink. In that moment Scarecrow and Mumfie fell upon him. They threw him on the ground, pummelling him with their truncheons, whilst the wretch shouted for mercy.

'You shall have mercy all right,' panted Scarecrow. 'Mumfie, find some cord, quick. I'll hold him down.'

Mumfie rushed out into the kitchen, and soon found a string bag hanging on the wall. He came back and together they tied up the struggling but rather dazed Secretary. They bound him so securely that he looked like a rather untidy black bundle.

'Now,' said Scarecrow, 'to the well with him. He shall help us to undo the professor.'

'Let me out of here,' cried the Secretary. Then he tried to wheedle. 'Come now, young gentlemen, let me out, I was only having a little game with you. Of course I would not really harm the old man.'

'Oh no!' said Scarecrow indignantly, 'I bet you wouldn't. Come on, Mumfie, we'll have to get him to the well somehow.'

135

They pulled him to his feet and drove him forward
through the garden towards the well, from which
feeble cries of 'Help!' could be heard.

'All right, professor dear,' called out Mumfie, 'we're
coming.' He ran forward to the well and peeped into
it. There half-way down was the professor sitting dis-
consolately in the bucket.

'Here we are,' Mumfie called down. 'Are you all
right?'

The professor called back feebly, 'Thank goodness
you've come. Make haste and draw me up, there's a
good animal. I am nearly frozen to death.'

They pushed the Secretary down upon the ground
and made him fast to a tree, then they hurried over to

the rope and began to haul up the professor. He was terribly heavy, and it was all they could do to get him to the top, but at last the bucket appeared and they made the rope fast. They helped out the poor old gentleman, who was so stiff that he could hardly stand up. They took him back to the cottage and sat him down in the chair at his desk with a rug over his knees, telling him that they would return in a few minutes. Then back to the well, where, untying the Secretary, they managed with a good deal of pulling and pushing to get him into the bucket, and the bucket over the side of the well. Then they lowered it half-way down until the rope secured to the table held it. They called down the well.

'There you are. And you can stay there for just as long as you made the professor, and we'll see how YOU like it. Perhaps you'll behave a good deal better when you come up again.'

The Secretary shook his fist at them. 'I'll get you for this,' he snarled. 'I'll make you suffer if it takes me . . .' But at that moment there was a creaking sound, the rope tautened and suddenly snapped. So sudden was it that they scarcely saw what had happened. The bucket, released, went careering down into the depths of the well. They could not see the bottom, but they heard a dull splash, and then all was quiet.

'Well,' said Scarecrow, 'I'm not sure that wasn't the best way after all. He was no use to anybody but himself.'

Mumfie climbed down and began dusting the cobwebs off his coat.

'Come along, Scarecrow,' he said happily. 'We'd better go and make the professor some soup; he'll need warming up a bit. Come to think of it, I'm a little bit chilly myself, are you, Scarecrow?'

'Yes, I am,' said Scarecrow. 'Are you sure you know how to make soup, Mumfie?'

'Oh yes,' said Mumfie, 'I've watched my Mummy make it lots of times. You just puts in everything you can find. Come along, Scarecrow, I'm hungry.'

They trotted off towards the cottage.

CHAPTER FIFTEEN

'I WONDER how that cord went and busted like that,' said Mumfie as they reached the front door. They ran inside and found the professor still sitting at his desk. He beamed at them as they ran over to him.

'Here you are. And very nice it is to see you again safe and sound. I was becoming quite worried about you before that extremely unpleasant individual came in. I cannot understand it, I found a piece of cord tied to the leg of my desk in the most untidy manner . . .'

'Oh, sir,' interrupted Mumfie and Scarecrow together, 'did you cut it?'

'Yes, I did, and to my surprise it flew straight out of the window. I cannot abide untidiness. But tell me how are you both, you certainly look none the worse for your adventures.'

'Oh, we're fine; but how are you, sir, I hope *you're* feeling none the worse for being down the well? We've got something lovely and exciting for you which will be sure to make you feel better.'

The old gentleman beamed at them. 'You don't tell me that you have actually found it? The goblin said that you were searching the palace, but I hardly thought . . .'

'Yes, we did,' said Mumfie and Scarecrow together. Mumfie fumbled in his pocket, trying to get out the magic box, which was rather a tight fit. He pulled it out and placed it triumphantly upon the professor's lap.

'Well, dear me, dear me,' said the professor, quite overcome. 'This is really – I must say this is really most affecting,' he sniffed. 'Be good enough to fetch me my reading glasses, you will find them on the mantelpiece. Well, well, this is such a momentous occasion that I find myself quite at a loss for words, quite at a loss. It is most remarkable – yes, yes, indeed.' He looked at

Mumfie over the top of his glasses, whilst Scarecrow went over to fetch his other pair. 'How very strange it is that the smaller people are, the more brains they appear to be blessed with. All the same I would hardly have thought it. Most remarkable,' he muttered again.

'Aren't you going to open it?' asked Mumfie excitedly. He was longing to see how the professor would open the magic box, and even more exciting still would be his first glimpse of real magic.

'Yes, I must open it at once. I only hope that it has not been tampered with, though I doubt if anyone but myself would ever find out how to open it. Let me see now, let me see. It's so long since I did it that I have almost forgotten the formula.' He gazed up at the ceiling, muttering strange words to himself under his breath. 'No, that wasn't it. Dear me, this is most distressing, most distressing. I am sadly out of practice. I used not to forget things like this.' He looked extremely worried.

'Oh dear,' said Mumfie. 'Wouldn't it be in one of your magic books, sir?'

'No, no, it isn't written down anywhere. You see, that would hardly be safe. If anyone were to come across it in a book then they would be able to open the box for themselves. I have been in the habit of closing my box with a short rhyme which I compose at the moment of shutting it. Only by reciting this rhyme can it be opened, and of course as I am the only person who knows it, only I can open the box.'

'My goodness!' cried Scarecrow, alarmed. 'You simply must remember it, sir; it's nearly night now and we haven't much time.'

At that moment there was a slight rustling sound from a small chair under the window.

'Hello,' squeaked Pinkey, getting up and flying over to the desk. 'You have been away a long time. I got tired of waiting for you, so I went to sleep. What are you all talking about?'

They explained to him about the box, and the difficulty the professor was experiencing in remembering how to open it.

'Oh, that,' said Pinkey. 'I remember the verse. I remember when you shut it, sir, I was sitting on the window-sill watching you. You looked up and saw me and you said, "That's it, I will make one up about Pinkey." I got excited to hear what you were going to make up about me so I listened most carefully.'

'Yes, yes!' they all cried together. 'But what did he say, Pinkey? Do hurry up.'

Pinkey flew up into the air, fluttering his wings and looking important. 'If I open it, do I get a piece of sugar cake?' he asked.

'Yes, indeed, you shall have the *whole* cake,' promised the professor hastily. 'Only please make haste.'

'Well, you ARE a pig,' said Scarecrow. 'Fancy thinking about food now.'

'Course I'm a pig,' sang Pinkey, flying round and round. He flew down on to the box and began,

> 'Pigs with wings fly round and round,
>   but wingless pigs stay on the ground.'

He had just got the last word out of his mouth when the lid of the box flew open with such a sudden pop that it shot him right on to the floor.

'Now do I get the cake?' he asked, picking himself up. But no one was taking the slightest notice of him; they were all gazing into the box.

Mumfie and Scarecrow watched fascinated, as one

by one seven tiny little men climbed out and lined up in a neat row on the table.

'Why, they're wooden soldiers!' said Mumfie, watching with surprise as they gradually grew bigger, until they stood nearly three inches high. 'Well, I never, who would have thought of such a thing, Scarecrow?'

But the professor signed to them to be quiet, and indeed it looked as though the small soldiers were eyeing them rather nervously.

'Now then. Number!' said the professor.

'One. Two. Three. Four. Five. Six. Seven,' cried the soldiers in surprisingly loud, military voices.

'All correct,' said the professor. 'Right about turn, back into the box quick march.'

The soldiers wheeled smartly and, gradually becoming smaller again, climbed back into the box, where they lay down in neat rows, four at the bottom, and three on top. It seemed to Mumfie that there was rather a struggle amongst them as to who should take the top places, but as soon as they were lying down you certainly would not know that they were anything but ordinary wooden soldiers like the ones he played with at home.

'Are you going to shut it up again?' he asked hopefully.

'Yes, we will close it and take it along with us at once. Let me see now. Dear me, it's very hard at times to think of a suitable verse.'

'Perhaps we could help,' said Mumfie. 'You think of something, Scarecrow. It would be fun to make up a real magic verse.'

'Yes, yes,' said the professor, 'I would welcome your assistance. Really, my brains seem to have become quite rusty.' He paced about the room making up the first lines of several verses to himself.

' 'Urry up!' said a deep voice from the box. 'It's getting cold in here.'

'All right, sergeant, all right. We will not be long.' The professor went on pacing.

'Well, this is a nice time of the day to go making up poems, and me all empty,' murmured Scarecrow. He wished that he could make up a magnificent poem on the spur of the moment, but his head was quite empty of ideas.

'Will this do?' asked Mumfie suddenly. He had been sitting quietly in a corner, staring out of the window:

'Professor lost his magic box
an' Scarecrow lost Mumfie.
Mumfie found the magic box,
So now we're all comfy.'

'Awful,' said Scarecrow, 'I mean,' as he saw Mumfie's face fall, 'I mean the rhyme's awful, but the idea's all right. Don't you think so, sir? But you ought to have said something about my finding you again, otherwise we shouldn't all have been comfy.'

'Well,' said the professor, 'the English is not all that could be desired; however, I think it very clever of you to have composed anything at all after the stress we have been through. I shall certainly use it. In fact, if you cared to, you might recite it, yourself. Put one finger on the lid, and mind that you do not forget the verse half-way through, because that would make it jam.'

Mumfie, beaming with pride, went over to the box.

He put one finger on the lid and recited the verse with a good deal of expression and feeling. As the lid snapped to, Scarecrow broke into loud applause to make up for his first rather carping remarks.

'Now we had really better hurry, sir, if you don't mind,' said Scarecrow, reluctantly abandoning the idea of soup, which he decided would have to wait until later. 'I'm afraid the others will be thinking we have been captured. We had better take the lantern, sir, it's quite dark outside.'

The professor agreed, and went out into the kitchen to fetch the lantern. Pinkey offered to carry it, flying just ahead of them. They went out of the cottage, and down the path that led to the tree.

CHAPTER SIXTEEN

AS they approached the tree they were greeted by an army of excited goblins. Alfie rushed forward and hugged Mumfie. 'Oh, we're so glad you've come, we were beginning to wonder what had happened to you. Is everything all right?'

'Everything's lovely,' said Mumfie. 'The professor has opened his magic box and nothing has been tampered with.'

He caught sight of a pale pink figure in the background. 'Oh, Pinkey,' he called, 'do stop wobbling the lantern about. I believe I can see your mama over there.'

But Pinkey had evidently seen the same thing. With

a shriek of delight he flew over the heads of the crowd.

'Quick! quick!' Mumfie pushed after him. 'I do wish I could fly. Oh, do move please, I want to watch how pleased Mrs. Pig will be when she sees him.'

He was just able to make his way through the crowd in time to see a most affecting sight. Mrs. Pig was holding the excited Pinkey in her arms, kissing and hugging him. She was laughing and crying at the same time with happiness, patting him, and tidying his wings, calling him her baby and her darling, all in one breath. Mumfie turned round to Scarecrow, who was just behind him.

'OO, my!' he said. 'Isn't she pleased to see him! I really must go and see Mama after this adventure's over; it will be lovely to see her again.' Then he remembered that of course poor Scarecrow had not got a mama so would be feeling rather out of this conversation.

He took hold of his hand and squeezed it. 'Of course you'll come too, Scarecrow. I couldn't possibly go without you, and she'll be ever so pleased to see you.'

Scarecrow grinned. 'I think that would be a fine idea. But in the meantime I really must get things organized or all these people will find themselves back as dreams before we know where we are. Come along, Professor,' he called. 'Can you make that magic? I think some of the people are beginning to look a bit dreamy. Bread, pull yourself together, there's a good fellow.'

'Dear me, yes,' said the professor. 'I shall have, of course, to go up on to the hill again.'

'But isn't that a very long way?' said Mumfie. 'It will take us ever such a time to get there, and there are all those goblins and guards still about in the wood.'

'That is easily managed,' smiled the professor. 'There will be no need for us to walk. I shall just make a magic that will carry us there in the speediest manner possible. Might I have a little less noise, please? It is really quite difficult for me to collect my thoughts with all this chattering going on.'

Scarecrow held up his hand and called for silence.

'Silence for the professor! The professor wants to think.'

The noise died away into a respectful silence as the crowd gathered round the old gentleman, who had sat down upon a tree-stump, the magic box upon his knees.

'Would you mind reciting the verse?' He turned to Mumfie, who was waiting expectantly. There was an awed hush in which you could have heard a pin drop, as Mumfie proudly recited his little verse.

No sooner had he done so than the box flew open and the seven soldiers climbed out, saluting smartly.

'Now, sergeant, pay careful attention,' said the professor. He flapped his arms in the air like birds' wings, then he pointed to himself, to Mumfie, and to Scarecrow, and said,

'Arble Barble Butterscotch and Marble,
Uppity Buppity Stumble and Bumpkin.'

'Right, sir,' said the sergeant. He gave an order to his men and then marched them back into the box. He climbed in himself, pulling the lid down after him.

'Do I have to say the verse again?' whispered Mumfie.

'Sh!' said the professor. 'Not whilst the magic is working.' He was putting the box back into his pocket.

As Mumfie watched him he felt the strangest sensation. He looked down and saw that his feet were leaving the ground. Gently, as though he were a feather, he was lifted up into the air. It was the loveliest feeling. He chuckled with delight as he watched Scarecrow rise slowly up off the ground in the wake of the professor, whose black coat blew out behind him. As they sailed up amongst the tree-tops there was a lusty cheer from the people below.

'Oo, Scarecrow, isn't this fun!' sang Mumfie. 'I've always wanted to fly all by myself, without any broom or umbrella or nuffing. Wasn't it kind of the professor to take us too!'

They looked down below them, to see that they had left the forest behind and were flying above smooth grassland, across which the now risen moon shed her gentle light. The little cottages and farms looked strangely sad and deserted with no warm lights in any of their windows. Mumfie thought how happy everyone would be to be able to spend the night in their own cosy beds, instead of floating about as dreams. They were now flying towards a high hill. The professor, who was leading the way, began to descend. Mumfie felt himself slipping down through the cool air until at last his feet touched the earth. They were standing on top of the moon-bathed hill, just underneath a thorn bush.

The professor looked solemn. Making a sign to them to be silent, he put the magic box down under the bush and walked three times round it. Then he beckoned to Mumfie, who crept forward, and placing his finger on the box, whispered the opening magic. The professor stood with arms outstretched as one by one the soldiers came quietly out. They flew up into the air and stood in a row before him.

'Now listen carefully,' ordered the professor.

He stooped towards the sergeant, whispering words so low that Mumfie and Scarecrow could not hear what he said. They watched the sergeant expectantly as he formed the soldiers into a ring. Then the professor took a match-box from his pocket and gave a match to each of the soldiers, which they held aloft like spears. He struck his own match, which burst into a bright blue flame. Immediately, and without any movement from the men, seven bright flames burst from the ends of their matches. The flames grew and grew until they

made a ring of fire which lit the whole sky so that the land was bright as day.

'Call the Dream Shapes!' cried the professor in a loud voice.

The lights flickered and grew dim, and as they watched, strange floating shapes mingled with the air, grey shapes without substance, softly floating until they hovered above the waning light. Mumfie was surprised to see many that he recognized. Bread, a shadow loaf, almost transparent. The billowing airy outline of Mrs. Pig, the farmer's wife and her five children, moulded together out of mist; they were all there, floating aimlessly round the professor.

'Are they all assembled?' he asked presently.

'All present and correct, sir,' said the sergeant.

'Then disperse the Dreams.'

Immediately there was a scrambling, rushing, pattering sound, and up the hill came bobbing and winking and gleaming, a small procession of friendly warm lights.

'Oh, look!' cried Mumfie delightedly, 'they're babies, and they're all carrying Night-lights.'

The children came running, dancing and hopping, each carrying his night-light in a bright pink saucer. They crowded round the professor, pushing each other to get a better view, and twittering like a flock of sparrows.

Mumfie jumped up and down. He looked up into the sky which was lit by the warm night-lights, trying to find the dreams, but they had all disappeared; indeed, it seemed hard to believe that they had ever been there.

'Scarecrow,' he whispered, 'I did see all those dreams floating about up there, didn't I?'

'I don't know,' said Scarecrow. 'You must have, I think, because I saw them too, but I was just beginning to wonder the same thing myself. I feel just as though I had been dreaming and had woken up and couldn't remember what it was all about.' He stopped as he felt someone tugging at his coat.

'Hello!' said a small voice, and he looked down to see one of the night-light babies smiling up at him.

'Oh hello!' he said, pleased. 'Of course I saw you in Night's garden when you were playing hide-and-seek. I don't think you ever told me your name?'

'Winkey,' said the baby. 'And that one over there is Twinkey. I wonder what will happen to Night's lovely garden now. Perhaps now the Secretary's gone she will be able to do what she likes with it again. Do you think so, sir?'

He turned to the professor, who was having a friendly conversation with some of the babies.

'I don't see what is to stop her,' answered the professor. 'I really think we had better see the poor lady and inform her as to the course which events have taken. She may not yet be aware of the fate which has befallen her Secretary.'

'Shall I collect the magics for you?' asked Mumfie hopefully. The soldiers were still hovering in the air, and he had noticed that they were looking a bit strained with the effort.

'Why dear me, yes,' said the professor. 'In the excitement of the moment they had temporarily slipped from my mind. If you would be so good.'

Mumfie marched over to the soldiers.

'ATTENTION!' he bellowed.

The soldiers came smartly to attention.

'DISMISS!'

' 'Ere,' said the sergeant. 'You can't do that.'

'Why not!' said Mumfie indignantly. 'That's what they say in the Navy anyway. I know 'cos I'm an Admiral in the Navy, so I can't be wrong. Can I, Scarecrow?' he added doubtfully.

'Of course not,' said Scarecrow. 'Ask him what he means.'

'What I mean is that if you dismiss them, they'll think you don't need them any more, and then they won't go back into the box.'

'Oh dear, that would never do,' said Mumfie, puzzled. 'Perhaps they do things different in the army.'

'If I might suggest it,' said the sergeant, 'it would be much appreciated if you were to give the men some leave.' He looked anxiously at his watch.

'What's he looking at his watch for?' asked Mumfie.

'I don't know. To see if they're still open, I expect,' suggested Scarecrow rather mysteriously.

The sergeant beamed. 'Got it in one, sir. May we go, sir?'

'Yes,' said Scarecrow. 'Tell them they are granted one hour's leave, Mumfie.'

'DISMISS FOR ONE HOUR'S LEAVE!' roared Mumfie. 'And see that you are back in the box as soon as whatever it is is closed again,' he added in a warning voice.

The soldiers all fell out and began running down the hill with remarkable speed. Mumfie watched them until they were out of sight, then he poked Scarecrow.

'Scarecrow,' he whispered. 'I do hope there's going to be some sort of celebration.'

'So do I,' said Scarecrow. 'And I hope it will include a little food, I don't know when I've been so hungry. But I'm afraid it isn't quite our position to suggest it.'

'Look, there's someone running up the hill. It looks like – why, I believe it is.'

'Is what?' said Scarecrow, who had been looking hopefully at the professor.

'It's Alfie,' said Mumfie, and ran down the hill to meet him.

Alfie was red in the face from his efforts. 'Important message,' he puffed. 'I must deliver it to the professor before I forget it.'

He ran up to the professor, Mumfie close behind him.

'I have a message for you, sir, from Night,' said Alfie importantly. There was a hush as everyone stopped to listen.

'She said—' Alfie took a deep breath. 'She said I was to thank you all very much for your wonderful efforts on her behalf, and she particularly wants to see Mumfie and Scarecrow and you, sir, and me, and she says she will be very pleased if you will all come to a party at the palace tomorrow night. And she says since none of you have had any sleep for such a long time she suggests that you all go back and have a good sleep now, and she'll see that you really enjoy it, so that you're fresh for the party tomorrow.'

He sounded quite puffed. 'Oh dear, I think that was all, but it was a dreadfully long message.'

'She didn't mention anything about food, I suppose?' suggested Scarecrow hopefully.

'No, I don't think so. But you can't have a really good party without food, can you, and I believe Night's parties are always good. Fireworks and all that.' He jumped about.

'Oh, my goodness,' said Mumfie suddenly. 'Look at the professor, the poor thing's tired out.'

Indeed, the professor was so fatigued after his strenuous efforts that he had fallen asleep under the thorn bush and was snoring gently.

'We'd better take him home,' said Scarecrow. 'Come

on, Mumfie, you look a bit sleepy yourself.' He yawned.

'Oh, bother,' said Mumfie, 'I wish I hadn't let the soldiers go, then he could make a magic to take us all back again. It's a terribly long way to walk.'

'Oh, that,' said Scarecrow, 'that's easy.' He stood up and bellowed at the top of his lungs,

> 'Arble Barble Butterscotch and Marble,
> Uppity Buppity Stumble and Bumpkin.
> Alfie, Professor, Mumfie and Me.'

'That's what comes of a good memory,' he said as they were gently lifted off the earth, without even waking the sleeping professor.

'But, Scarecrow, however did you manage it?' said Mumfie with admiration.

'Training,' replied Scarecrow grandly. 'William the Conqueror, 1066 and all that sort of thing.'

'Oh,' said Mumfie, 'I see.'

They were over the forest again, and soon they were gently deposited in front of the professor's cottage. They put the old gentleman to bed and then went into the kitchen, where they made a very good supper of cold chicken and pickles. They climbed on to the kitchen settle, and were soon fast asleep.

CHAPTER SEVENTEEN

MUMFIE rubbed his eyes, and sat up. He looked round for Scarecrow, who should have been on the settle beside him.

'Oh dear, oh dear, he must have fallen off in the night. Poor Scarecrow.'

Sure enough, Scarecrow was lying on the floor, his

head pillowed on his hat. He grunted as Mumfie leant over and tickled his nose.

'Eh? What? What is it? Where am I? It's hard.'

'Wake up, Scarecrow, it's a lovely sunny day. We'll make the professor's breakfast as a surprise.'

Mumfie washed himself under the tap, but Scarecrow was too busy cutting the rind off the bacon, to bother.

'I shall have to wash later on for the party, anyhow.'

'That's a delicious smell you're making, Scarecrow,' said Mumfie presently as the bacon sizzled in the pan. He found some eggs in the larder, and a couple of tomatoes. He cracked the eggs into a cup and poured them carefully into the pan. 'Can you eat two, Scarecrow?'

'I certainly can,' said Scarecrow. 'And you'd better do two for the professor, but only one for yourself. You're fat enough as it is.'

'All right,' agreed Mumfie. 'But I shall do myself a piece of fried bread, and I shall have most of the tomatoes.'

At that moment the professor came in. He looked much refreshed from his night's sleep, and declared that he had not slept so well for a long time.

'Dear me, this is very pleasant,' he said, as he saw the breakfast neatly laid on the kitchen table. When they had finished, Mumfie ran out into the orchard to say good morning to Mrs. Pig.

Pinkey flew out in a great state of excitement and a clean pinafore. 'Come inside,' he squeaked. 'Mama will be ever so pleased to see you.'

They found Mrs. Pig busily trying on her best hat before the mirror. 'There!' she cried, 'I looked it out for the party. Isn't it a love?'

'Charming,' said Scarecrow gallantly. 'Quite charming.'

'I like the roses in the front,' said Mumfie. 'What are we going to wear for the party, Scarecrow? We both looks a bit shabby. I do wish I hadn't torn my coat.'

'Well, that's easily dealt with,' said Mrs. Pig comfortably; she sent them off to play with the pig children whilst she mended the tear. They had such fun that the day simply flew. Lunch-time, tea-time, then a rest before getting ready for the party.

Mumfie was busy resting by getting right down to the bottom of the professor's bed and pretending to be a rabbit, when there was a knock at the cottage door.

'I'd better go,' said Scarecrow. 'The professor's probably busy.' He slipped out of bed, and opened the

front door. Outside was a small girl whose face he seemed to have seen before.

'Hello!' she said. 'Is Mumfie there?'

'Yes,' said Scarecrow. 'Come in. He's just having a nap. What have you got inside those boxes?'

'I don't know; they're for you. Night sent me along with them.'

'Oo, my!' said Scarecrow. 'Mumfie, here's someone to see you.' Mumfie bounced out of bed.

'Hello!' he said. 'It's nice to see you again. Though you said we never should.'

'Yes,' said the child. 'And I didn't think so either after I'd left you with the Secretary. It was terribly clever of you and your friend to find the professor's magic. Night is ever so happy. She can enjoy herself in the garden now. Of course she's been asleep all day, but she was getting up just before I left, and she's making the garden simply lovely for the party. I mustn't stay though or I won't have time to get ready myself. Look, she sent these for you.' She put down the two boxes on the bed.

'Oo, aren't they pretty!' said Mumfie, looking at the bright transparent paper and coloured ribbons. 'Which is mine?'

'They've got your names on them. I really must fly now – see you at the party.'

They saw her to the door, and watched her flit through the wood, then they rushed back to open their parcels.

'I do love a present,' sighed Mumfie. 'This is mine. Look, it says "Mumfie" on the label – I wonder what it is.'

He undid the ribbon and the paper, folding them carefully, then he pulled off the lid. He dived inside the

box and pulled out a beautiful curly ten-gallon stetson
hat, a gay red shirt, scarf, cartridge belt, chaps; in fact,
everything to make up a really correct cowboy outfit.
Stuck into the hat brim was a tiny card, and on it was
written in silver ink, 'For Mumfie to dress up in at the
party.'

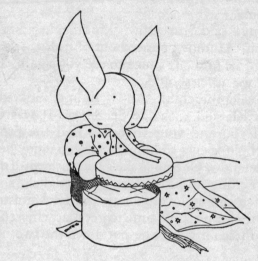

Mumfie whooped with delight. 'Oo, Scarecrow, just
look what I've got. What's in yours?'

'Same,' said Scarecrow happily, putting on his stetson hat at a most rakish angle. 'Only my shirt's blue.
How do I look?'

'Fine,' said Mumfie admiringly. He thought the
shirt was just the colour of Scarecrow's eyes, but did
not say so for fear of annoying him. He hoped that he
would manage to look equally dashing in his stetson.
He put it on very much over one ear, leaving the
other one sticking out, but decided that this was not
very comfortable, so he tucked in the other ear,

scrambled into the suit and climbed up to look at himself in the glass.

'You look fine,' said Scarecrow. 'Just like Buffalo Bill himself. I must get into the rest of my things – it must be almost time to start. I do hope we can find our way to the tree all right,' he added doubtfully.

'Oh, Alfie said he'd come to fetch us,' said Mumfie. 'I wonder if everybody will be in fancy dress?'

'Mrs. Pig won't. She'll just be in a hat. There's somebody outside now – I wonder if it's Alfie.

'Hello, Alfie, you do look smart. Just wait a minute while we finish getting ready.'

Alfie was so cleaned and polished that he positively shone. He had on a clean blue tunic, and his best leather jacket. His red acorn hat was perched jauntily on the back of his head. He gazed at Mumfie and Scarecrow with the greatest admiration.

'My! what a fine pair of suits,' he said. 'Wherever did you get them? Oh, look – here's the professor. Good evening, sir.'

The professor came into the room, brushing up his best hat.

'Well, I think we had better make a start,' he said. 'I think the Pig family are outside, so we will all go along together.'

The pigs were all very squeaky and excited, with Mrs. Pig looking very charming in her new hat. She introduced Mumfie and Scarecrow to her husband, who proved to be the most enormous pig that they had ever seen. Mumfie admired him very much, and hoped that he would be able to get as fat as that one day. He liked him better still when with a friendly grunt he offered a ride as far as the tree. Mumfie scrambled up on to his back and pretended that he was on a bucking bronco. He let out wild whoops as they went along.

When they arrived at the tree the door was open, and a bright light glowed from inside. The goblins had evidently been very busy, for the passage and stairway were lit with many lanterns, so that they looked gay and cheerful. When they reached the passage that turned off towards the cells Mumfie suggested that they should go and fetch the old gaoler.

'There won't be anyone in prison now, so he might as well come to the party.'

The old toad was sitting on a stool looking rather lonely.

'Come along, Jimmy,' said Mumfie. 'We've come to fetch you to the party.'

'Eh?' croaked the toad. 'Me at a party – not likely. Never been to a party in me life – and not going to start now. Me at a party. The very idea!'

'Come on,' said Mumfie and Scarecrow and Alfie, catching hold of him. 'It will do you good.'

'Yes,' said Scarecrow. 'See life, and brush up your ideas.'

The passage outside was crowded with gob-

lins and other people all making their way to the party. The old toad was at last persuaded into coming along, though not without a good deal of grumbling and muttering.

People stood respectfully on one side to let the professor pass, and Mumfie realized from all their friendly and delighted greetings, how very fond of him they must be. They arrived at last at the garden door where one of the guards, looking very smart in a bright new uniform, asked to see their invitation cards.

Mumfie looked round at Scarecrow in dismay.

'But, Scarecrow,' he whispered. 'We didn't have any invitation cards, and look, he won't let anyone through without.'

The professor was fumbling in his pocket, from which he produced a small white card, which he handed

absent-mindedly to the guard, who saluted smartly and passed him through the door.

'Whatever are we to do?' cried Mumfie, as people started to push by them.

'Come along, please,' said the guard, looking at them rather severely. 'Pass along and make way for those behind you. Cards, please.'

'But we haven't got any cards,' began Mumfie dolefully.

'Then what's that in yor 'ats?' asked the guard.

Mumfie and Scarecrow felt in their hats, and took out the cards that had been with their parcels.

'That's right,' said the guard, taking them and hurrying them along before they had time to say anything.

He pushed them through the gate and into a moonlit fairyland more lovely than anything Mumfie had ever seen.

CHAPTER EIGHTEEN

'OH look, Scarecrow!' said Mumfie in wonderment. 'She must have taken all those stars from their cases and hung them about everywhere.' He pointed to the trees, which were spangled with thousands of stars that glittered through the garden, shedding their enchanting light amongst the flowers and over the excited throng of guests, who were making their way towards the palace. As they went along, Scarecrow noticed several of the Moonbeams, who carried baskets from which they were throwing handfuls of Stardust, so that the grass sparkled under their feet.

When they reached the palace Night was standing on the steps waiting to greet them.

'Ah, here are my guests of honour.' She smiled down

at them. She shook hands with Scarecrow, who took off his hat and made her a deep bow, then she picked Mumfie up and gave him a kiss. Mumfie beamed at her.

'Thank you very much for the suit, ma'am,' he said shyly. 'I've always wanted a cowboy suit.'

'Yes, madam, thank you very much,' said Scarecrow. 'Look at my belt, it's got two pistols in it.' He pulled them out proudly.

'I'm glad you like them,' smiled Night. 'You both make very fine cowboys.' She turned to the professor, who was looking benignly at the company in general.

'Come up to the gallery with me,' she invited him. 'I'm sure the children are all longing to begin playing. Oh, Mrs. Pig, what a charming hat. You could not have found anything more becoming.'

Mrs. Pig, who was waiting with her family at the foot of the steps, blushed with pleasure. She bobbed a curtsy, and peeped round to see whether her husband had heard the compliment.

Then Night held up her hand for silence.

'I think we had better begin with the surprises,' she said. 'There is one for each of you – they are all hidden about in the garden – different coloured packets with your name on each. There will also be a prize for the first one to find his or her packet. We will be watching you from the gallery, and I shall ask the professor to blow on his whistle when it is time to start.'

She collected all the grown-ups and took them up with her to the gallery that overlooked the garden.

Mumfie bounced about. 'Scarecrow, isn't this lovely! I do hope I find my packet first.'

The professor at a sign from Night blew a long blast upon his whistle. Mumfie and Scarecrow dashed off together and began searching about amongst the bushes and flowers.

'Hello,' called Alfie, rushing by. 'They say the Moon's coming to the party later on. I'm going to look down by the lily pond. Cheero!'

Pinkey was flying about peeping amongst the branches of a tree. 'This tree's full of pigeons,' he called down. 'They've got a nest here, and I'm sure one of them's sitting on my parcel.'

'Well, I don't know my way about very well,' said Scarecrow, 'so I think I shall look in the tool-shed – Night knows I've been in there, so it's quite a likely place. Where will you look, Mumfie?'

'I don't know.' Mumfie was a little puzzled. 'I think I shall go down this little path; it looks rather exciting.'

'All right. See you later.' Scarecrow ran off towards the tool-shed.

Mumfie went along the path until presently it became quite quiet. It was evident that no one else had thought of looking here. He came to the end, which led down to the edge of a wide lake. By the water's edge was moored a small blue boat.

'Oo, what an exciting place,' said Mumfie to himself.

He went over to the boat and climbed inside. As he looked across the lake his eyes opened wide with surprise, for a long ray of light came down from the sky, landing in the water.

'Why, it's a ladder!' cried Mumfie. 'Coming right down out of the sky.' He looked up to see where it was coming from, and there above hung the pale crescent moon. As he watched, something very odd seemed to be happening up there. It looked just as though someone were climbing out. Yes, he could distinctly see whoever it was swing his legs over the crescent and start to climb down the ladder. He waited breathless as the figure came nearer and nearer. Oh, how he gleamed and shone as he swung gracefully down. Mumfie held his breath with excitement.

'Oh, look out, sir!' he called suddenly. 'You'll be in the water!'

The man on the ladder stopped, and the shining cord swayed out over the lake.

'Oh dear,' he said, 'that was a bad shot. I thought I'd dropped it over the land.'

Mumfie jumped out of the boat and began to push it down into the water. He climbed in and took up the oars.

'Wait a minute,' he called. 'I'll row out to you.'

He was so excited that he caught a good many crabs, and once nearly lost the oars, but he managed to bring the boat under the foot of the ladder.

The shining man dropped lightly down.

'That's very good of you,' he said. 'I hope I'm not late for the party?'

'Oh no, your Majesty,' said Mumfie, hoping that was the right way to address him. He tried to row as neatly as possible. 'It's only just begun. We heard you might be coming. Oh dear!' he said as he scrambled out of the boat. 'I quite forgot to look for my parcel and now I shall probably be last.' He looked rather forlorn.

'I bet you won't,' said the Moon. 'Come on, I'll give you a pick-a-back, then you can look for it as you go along – you'll find it much easier to see now.' He swung Mumfie up on to his shoulder.

'This is fun!' cried Mumfie. 'You does make everything bright, sir; it was quite dark along this path

when I came. Oh wait a minute, please, I'm sure I can
see a parcel on that branch. Yes it is – it's *my* parcel –
it's got MUMFIE on the label. Let's hurry, please. I
might be first after all.'

The Moon started to run, he ran very swiftly out into
the clearing towards the palace steps, Mumfie riding
on his shoulder and waving the red parcel in the air. As
they approached the steps he saw that there was someone ahead of them – Scarecrow, lean and rakish in his
cowboy clothes, dashing up the steps, a blue parcel in
his hand. Mumfie tugged at the Moon's shoulder.

'Wait a minute,' he whispered. 'That's Scarecrow.
Let him be first.'

The Moon laughed and put him down. 'There
you are. Hurry up and you'll just about make a tie of
it.'

Mumfie bumbled off, but his legs were too short to

catch up with Scarecrow. He arrived rather puffed, a good second.

Scarecrow was handing his present to the professor, who, recognizing him, beamed at him through his spectacles. He raised Scarecrow's arm in the air and called, 'The Winner!'

'And me second,' piped Mumfie excitedly. 'Mumfie second, professor.'

All the others were now beginning to come in. Alfie tied for third place with one of the Night-light babies. They all stood aside as the Moon strode up on to the balcony. He bowed gallantly to Night, and sat down beside her. Then she beckoned to Scarecrow to come up and get his prize. Amid a good deal of clapping and cheering she presented him with a beautiful electric torch.

Scarecrow grinned all over his face with pleasure.

'Thank you very much, ma'am. It's just what I've always wanted.' He ran down to show it to Mumfie, who spent a good time turning it on and off, and flashing it at everybody. Then they sat down to open their parcels.

'Did you see me riding on the Moon's shoulder?' whispered Mumfie proudly. 'What's in your parcel?'

'It's a penknife!' whooped Scarecrow. 'With four different blades.' He slipped it in his pocket. 'What have you got, Mumfie?'

'Balloons,' said Mumfie happily. 'A whole packet of them. Have you got any string, Scarecrow?'

Scarecrow found some string in his pocket, and Mumfie blew up a big red balloon and tied it on to the back of his hat. He thought this very funny, and ran about with it bobbing behind him.

Alfie ran up, waving a gaily coloured flag. 'Look

what I've got. Come on, everyone's going inside for the feast. I wonder if there'll be ices.'

They trooped into the palace, across the courtyard where the fountain played, and into a great hall gaily hung with flowers, where a wonderful feast was spread. Each place was marked with a tiny name-card. Attendants made their way amongst the guests, helping them to find their places.

'I can't find me anywhere,' said Mumfie, when he had been up and down each side of the table. 'And I can't find Scarecrow. Oh dear, I do hope they haven't forgotten us.'

By now people had found their seats, and were waiting for Night to take the head of the table.

She came in on the professor's arm, and looking round the room called to Mumfie and Scarecrow to come up and sit between her and the Moon in the places of honour.

Mumfie scrambled up into his seat, and beamed round upon the company. He peeped at the professor, who sat at Night's right hand, with Alfie just beyond him. Scarecrow sat next to the Moon, and hoped that he would not notice how much he was going to eat.

It was a wonderful meal, with all the nicest things imaginable; even strawberries and cream, and to end up with, a wonderful iced pudding covered with magic stars and silver bobbles that melted in a delicious manner when you put them in your mouth.

Scarecrow drank a good deal of ginger beer, whilst Mumfie chose a very pink raspberry drink that fizzed attractively. He had four ices, and a good many chocolate cakes. When everyone had finished, Night called upon the professor to make a speech.

'Dear me, dear me,' said the old gentleman, peering through his glasses, and fumbling in his pocket for the speech, which he had carefully written out. He rose, and, clearing his throat, began:

'Ladies and gentlemen. I have much pleasure in taking this opportunity of thanking my two little friends for their remarkable courage and gallantry during their successful efforts to find my magic box. (Cheers.) And I think I may speak for us all when I say that they saved this island from the clutches of the grasping Secretary; a person of such deplorable character that I fear his end can call for but passing regret. (Cheers.) I am sure that we are all delighted to see Night once more in full possession of her own domain; freed from the interferences of an ambitious

servant, who, had he fulfilled his duties without over-stepping them, might have been here with us this evening, happily partaking of that delicious iced pudding. (Loud cheers.)

'Well, I do not propose to weary you with a long speech, and so I will close, by proposing a toast.'

He raised his glass and called, 'To Night, our charming hostess.' The toast was drunk with much enthusiasm and clinking of glasses. Scarecrow hastily popped another bottle of ginger beer – he was afraid that if there were to be many more toasts he would have nothing to drink them in.

Night had risen, and was thanking them all. She held up her hand for silence.

'And now, I will call a toast,' she said. 'To our guests of honour, and the heroes of the day, Mumfie and Scarecrow.'

There was a storm of cheering, people rising in their seats to drink the toast. Mumfie picked up his raspberry pop, and was about to drink enthusiastically, when Scarecrow kicked him under the table, frowning at him severely.

'What's the matter?' whispered Mumfie, under cover of the applause.

'You mustn't drink your own toast,' said Scarecrow. 'It's most awful bad manners; I'm surprised at you, Mumfie.'

Mumfie thought this a pity, but he smiled round happily at the assembled company as there were cries of 'Speech! Speech! Let's hear Mumfie and Scarecrow.'

'Go on, Scarecrow!' Mumfie poked him. 'They wants a speech.'

'Not me!' said Scarecrow, firmly burying his face in his ginger beer. 'That sort of thing is not at all in my line. You say something, Mumfie, you'll be much better at it. I'll help you if you get stuck.'

'Oh my,' said Mumfie. 'Oh dear, I wish I didn't feel quite so full.'

He stood up on his chair, and bowed politely to the company.

'Ladies and gentlemen, and the Professor,' he began, hoping that this was the right way to start. 'I think this is a lovely party, specially the strawberries and cream, and the Moon coming.' He smiled round at the Moon, who bowed in acknowledgement of the compliment.

'Scarecrow and me enjoyed finding the professor's magic – didn't we, Scarecrow? – and meeting Alfie and Mrs. Pig and everyone, and seeing the professor open his magic box with the poem I made up; and

181

thank you very much for the lovely party, and my balloons, and Scarecrow's torch – and please may I get down now?' He scrambled down off his chair, and up on to the Moon's knee, where he listened happily to the storms of applause.

'Did I make a good speech?' he asked.

'Very good,' smiled the Moon, tweaking his ear. 'My goodness, what's going on down there!' For a commotion had broken out at one end of the table. Pinkey who had eaten far too many pink sugar cakes and was blown out to quite twice his natural size, was now discovered in the middle of the iced pudding having a bad attack of hiccups. He was hauled out of the bowl by his brothers and sisters and carried over to the window to be patted on the back and given as much air as possible. Mrs. Pig, her hat very much on one side, was fanning him with her handkerchief until he gradually recovered enough to fall sound asleep, clutching a wooden horse that he had found in the garden.

When Night saw that nothing really serious had happened, she suggested that they should all go out into the garden again, where the Moonbeams were to dance for them.

Mumfie looked very excited. He poked Scarecrow. 'Do you think she'll be there?' he whispered.

'I expect so. I wonder if the professor knows.'

Mumfie ran up to Night and pulled at her skirt to catch her attention.

'Excuse me,' he said shyly, 'but is the professor's granddaughter going to dance with the Moonbeams?'

'Why yes, of course. She will be leading the dancers. It will be nice for him to see how she is getting on.'

'Yes,' said Mumfie doubtfully. 'Is she always going to be a Moonbeam?'

'Why naturally,' said Night, surprised. 'Why do you ask?'

'Well, I was just wondering,' said Mumfie bravely. ' 'Cos Mrs. Pig said the professor missed her badly, and

183

she did say herself that she'd rather be an ordinary little girl at home in the professor's garden. Oh dear,' he finished, rather confused. 'P'r'aps I shouldn't have said that.'

But Night was smiling at him kindly. She turned to the Moon, who was standing by her side.

'I wonder why the silly little thing didn't tell me? We'll let them do their dance, and then we will look into the matter.' She patted Mumfie on the head, and watched him as he trotted off to find Scarecrow. He sat down beside him on the grass, where the people had formed a wide ring in which the Moonbeams were to dance.

'Here they come!' cried Alfie excitedly, pointing up to the high tower which climbed up into the sky, to be lost in darkness. Down through the cool night air floated the Moonbeams in their lovely gleaming dresses. They were led by the beautiful girl of the tower. As she landed lightly on the grass Mumfie noticed that, unlike the others, her dress was embroidered with tiny pearls. She looked eagerly about her as though trying to find some familiar face in the crowd. Mumfie and Scarecrow looked at the professor, who was peering anxiously at the dancers as they whirled around, their flying skirts tracing graceful patterns against the dark trees.

'Do you like the dance?' Mumfie asked him.

'Charming! Charming!' said the professor, sitting back in his chair. 'Very pretty indeed. Unfortunately my sight is not so good as it was – I cannot see the children's faces very clearly.' He sighed.

'I think they're finishing now,' said Scarecrow, as the dancers swept in a deep curtsy before Night. Then they rushed towards the Moon, clustering round him,

so that their gleaming lights were caught up in his radiance.

'Come on and dance too,' they chorused. 'Come and dance with us, Moon.'

The Moon turned to Night. 'Do you mind if I dance?' he asked. 'It's really time that I was getting home – I've left the sky dark for quite long enough. I'll take the Moonbeams with me.'

'Oh dear,' whispered Mumfie. 'Did you hear that, Scarecrow? He said he was going to take the Moonbeams with him. Poor professor. It does seem a shame.'

The Moon sprang out upon the grass, he leapt high into the air and began to dance. Lighter than air he seemed, so that his feet did not touch the ground.

'Oh, look!' cried Mumfie. 'He's getting higher and higher up into the air, and the Moonbeams are going with him.'

The Moon soared up and up, gathering speed as he danced across the sky, so that presently he became indistinct – a glowing light from which spread the soft rays of the Moonbeams. At last he stopped dancing. The clear still crescent of the moon hung above them, shedding its pale light over the garden.

'I do wish she hadn't gone back,' said Scarecrow. 'We didn't even get a chance to speak to her.'

But Mumfie was looking at the professor, who, an expression of extreme delight upon his face, was talking to a little girl in a blue frock with a white pinafore.

'Scarecrow, who's that the professor is talking to? I'm sure I didn't see her before.' He looked up at the moon, and then back at the small girl in the pinafore.

Scarecrow looked at the fair shining hair, and was not deceived by the little girl's ordinary frock.

'That's the professor's granddaughter,' he said, giving a little skip into the air. 'Night must have allowed her to stay behind. Mumfie, I think we'd better be going now. This party has ended in a lovely way, and I can't help thinking about Selina, and how she will be missing us.'

'Yes,' agreed Mumfie, clutching his precious bag of balloons. 'I think we should be getting back now. Shall we go and say good-bye?'

They ran over to the professor.

'We really ought to be getting home, sir,' said Scarecrow. He grinned at the lovely child. 'I'm so glad you're going home again.'

'Yes, yes indeed,' said the professor happily. 'I think we should all be going home now. This has really been the most delightful evening. You will come back with us to the cottage, of course? The Pig family left a little while ago in order to get Pinkey back to bed.'

Mumfie poked Scarecrow. 'It's ever so kind of you, sir,' he said. 'But I think we'd better be getting back to Selina.' He yawned rather sleepily. 'Could you possibly make a magic, sir?'

'Why yes, of course. Let me see now, where is the box?'

He pulled it out of his pocket. Mumfie watched sleepily as the seven soldiers came out. 'Can I make the magic?' he asked.

The professor nodded.

'I should like a nice, warm, cotton-woolly sort of cloud to come down into the garden and take us home again,' he said. 'Oh, Scarecrow, I *do* wish I had a magic box all of my own.'

He climbed on to the cloud, which had drifted down into the garden. As it floated into the air he peeped down at the professor and his granddaughter, small figures below them, waving them out of sight. He turned round to Scarecrow, who had made himself quite comfortable, his head pillowed on his hat.

'Any further orders, sir?' said a loud military voice quite close to his ear.

'Oh dear,' said Mumfie. 'Did I forget to give you back to the professor?' He rubbed his eyes.

'No, sir, certainly not, sir,' said the sergeant. 'The professor said that we were to stay with you, sir.'

'Oh, Scarecrow!' sang Mumfie ecstatically.

He picked up the toy soldiers and put them carefully back into the box, then he snuggled close to Scarecrow and went to sleep.

THE END

MICHAEL BENTINE'S POTTY ADVENTURE BOOK

0 552 52060 8   40p

You can join the Potties as they set off in their time box to visit the old Wild West to see how good Wild Bill Hiccup really was with his gun.

You can travel back in history with Professor Crankpotts from Pottisdam University to discover how the 'lump of stone' really found its way to Westminster Abbey, underneath the Coronation Chair.

You can join Colonel 'Potty' Potterton and his 19th Pottistani Lancers as they hold the Gateway to India against the yelling hordes of the Mad Mullah.

MALCOLM SAVILLE'S COUNTRY BOOK

0 552 54030 7   30p

It is not necessary to go far into the countryside to find a whole new world awaiting exploration. Malcolm Saville tells you how to gain the most from a day at the farm, a quiet browse by a pond, or a stroll along the hedgerows or through a wood – and stresses that there is much to be found all the year round.

He also tells you how to recognize the wild flowers and trees of the countryside, to distinguish between the barley and the oats in the farmers' fields and to recognize the snuffling of a hedgehog. You will discover how much extra enjoyment can be had on a walk by using a compass or a map, how to picnic and how to camp, and even how to recognize the stars at night.

EAT WHAT YOU GROW BY MALCOLM SAVILLE

0 552 54075 7   30p

Have you ever eaten home-grown vegetables? They are delicious and don't necessarily need a lot of room. You can grow ridge cucumbers that start off in an egg box on a window ledge and mustard and cress which grows well on a flannel. You'll find many useful tips in this book.

If you would like to receive a newsletter telling you about our new children's books, fill in the coupon with your name and address and send it to:

Gillian Osband,
Transworld Publishers Ltd,
Century House
61-63 Uxbridge Road, Ealing,
London, W5 5SA

NAME ....

ADDRESS ....

....

....

CHILDREN'S NEWSLETTER

All the books on the previous pages are available at your bookshop or can be ordered direct from Transworld Publishers Ltd., Cash Sales Dept., P.O. Box 11, Falmouth, Cornwall.

Please send full name and address together with cheque or postal order – no currency, and allow 10p per book to cover postage and packing (plus 5p each for additional copies).